THE DEVIL AND THE
DOLCE VITA

By the same author

At the Lake of Sudden Death

THE DEVIL AND THE DOLCE VITA

Timothy Holme

Walker and Company
New York

For Bianca with love

Published in the United States of America
in 1988 by the Walker Publishing Company, Inc.

Library of Congress Cataloging-in-Publication Data

Holme, Timothy.
    The devil and the dolce vita.

    I. Title.
PR6058.045355D48 1988   823'.914   88-5525
ISBN 0-8027-5695-6

Printed in the United States of America

10 9 8 7 6 5 4 3 2 1

THE DEVIL AND THE DOLCE VITA

One

The helicopter made a wide u-turn over the lighthouse, then started to fly back down the fourteen-kilometre-long, dead straight beach of Jesolo lido which is Italy's number two seaside resort (coming after Rimini) and is situated just across the lagoon from Venice. On the wooden jetties which had been constructed at regular intervals to prevent the sea washing away the sand, holiday-makers lay sprawled in the September sun. At no less regular intervals were flag posts with limp blue pennons which indicated that you could safely swim; and in fact the sea was as motionless as a vast skating-rink.

'*Mamma mia!*' said the co-pilot from the Venetian harbour board police, looking through his binoculars. 'What a pair of legs!'

'You're meant to be looking for irregularities,' said the pilot, 'not girls.' But he, too, looked down to locate the girl; and they were flying low enough for him to be able to do so comfortably even without binoculars. Her legs were indeed magnificent; she was wearing a bikini which revealed a flat tummy and just about concealed hard, rather small, breasts; long fair hair fell straight down her back; she was probably not much more than fifteen.

As though she were aware of the pilots' scrutiny she waved up at the helicopter, smiling and shading her eyes with her other hand against the sun.

'There never are any irregularities in Jesolo,' said the co-pilot answering the original question.

'A German got drowned last week,' the pilot offered encouragingly.

'Oh, I don't count that,' said the co-pilot. 'That's part of the routine administration. I mean real irregularities. There's

7

something unnatural about Jesolo—like an indoor football pitch with plastic grass. No roots.'

Like a monstrous science fictional insect the helicopter droned its way along the beach. To its left stretched out the large, mostly ugly and strictly functional buildings which were the hotels and apartment blocks of Jesolo. This built-up area went all fourteen kilometres from the lighthouse to Jesolo village; but if it was long it was not broad. In fact, as you went inland from the sea it gave way almost immediately to long stretches of fields, dry and dusty, infected with insects and dotted here and there with oldish and sometimes dilapidated buildings.

The helicopter reached Jesolo village and, having made another wide u-turn, started back. The co-pilot looked down at the cluster of houses below.

'Nothing ever happens in Jesolo,' he said moodily.

Like many generalisations, that of the co-pilot was open to a vast exception. This exception was brewing and bubbling some sixty metres beneath them, and two people had, all unwittingly, got a line onto it. The first was a journalist . . .

Wendell Banner had the happy knack of turning out Reader's Digest style best-sellers. He had written one about great horse races, researching and analyzing each race in the minutest detail; another about famous disasters using the same technique.

He was now working on a book about five day wonders, the preparation of which had brought him to a restaurant-cum-*pizzeria* in Jesolo village called the Dolce Vita which a couple of years previously had been the scene of a five day wonder. And Wendell Banner had come to interview the man who had been at the centre of it.

Like all places which display frenetic merriment by night, the Dolce Vita looked a bit jaded in the morning. A handful of people were sitting under the awning outside enjoying, or at any rate eating, the prominently advertised "English Breackfast". A solitary waiter was leaning against the door which led into the restaurant proper looking at a newspaper and keeping an

8

occasional eye on the customers, rather like an absent-minded keeper in a wild life park checking on the animals.

'Captain Coliselli?' Banner enquired.

The waiter looked puzzled. Then understanding dawned. 'Captain Gigi you mean?' he said.

'That's right.'

'Daresay he's still in bed.'

'I've got an appointment with him.'

'Call him if you like,' offered the waiter, adding with absent-minded hospitality, 'Come in and sit down.'

They went past a large rostrum with music stands, microphone and drums, then through swing doors into the restaurant where the waiter waved Banner to a chair and went out through one of the two doors at the other end of the room.

Banner looked about him. Everywhere on the walls there hung framed newspaper cuttings and he went over to read one or two of the headlines. *Captain Gigi's Republic*, shouted one. *Jesolo to claim Independence?* asked another. *Free Jesolo Movement launched*, bawled a third.

There were also numerous photographs of the Captain. If you searched Italian naval records you would find them unhelpful concerning the source of this commission, but to make up for this Gigi Coliselli looked the part to a tee. His large, flabby countenance was both climaxed and crowned by a heavily braided naval officer's cap and his form, dominated by a huge and sagging belly at the front and mountainous buttocks at the rear, was clothed in impeccable naval uniform.

Banner already knew the outline of the story which had sent Captain Gigi soaring to the status of a five day wonder. Across the lagoon in Venice an elderly scholar had discovered and made public a document in which an eighteenth century doge had granted to a certain Giacomo Coliselli and his descendants in perpetuity the right to govern "Jesulum" as an independent state in return for hospitality received from the said Coliselli.

At first the document was regarded as little more than a curiosity, but then it emerged that Captain Gigi—backed by some of the larger property owners in Jesolo who saw enormous financial benefits in independent status—was taking

9

it in all seriousness. He hired lawyers to prove his descent from the eighteenth century Coliselli and staked his claim to governorship of Jesolo.

At this, if not exactly all Hell, at least all the Italian political scene broke loose. The government opposed Jesolan independence, arguing that it could not be held bound by a decision made by a Venetian doge before the unification of Italy. The Italian Communist Party and the rest of the opposition argued that San Marino had been independent long before the unification of Italy, but not for that was its independence rendered invalid.

The affair became a political labyrinth of an intricacy such as can only be attained in Italy. Every imaginable wile was practised, insults flew, headlines flared. *Time* magazine even ran a cover story on the affair. But the Italian prime minister at the time was even shrewder than most Italian prime ministers. He knew that in such situations waiting and winning are practically synonymous. And in fact before long the arguments were no longer really about Jesolo at all, but about who should get which job, which parties would form a temporary alliance, what government grants would be made to whom and when.

Gradually it dawned on Captain Gigi that it was all over and that he was left with nothing more substantial than a large pile of newspaper cuttings which he set about having framed, at the same time adjusting with bad grace to the return of obscurity.

All this Banner knew. What he wanted now was something to give flesh to the bare bones of the story and Captain Gigi who now entered the room had enough of this and to spare.

The previous evening as the Captain had weaved his way among the tables of the Dolce Vita, regally accepting a glass of wine here and dancing with a balloon-like German matron there, swinging the coloured lights as he went, he had looked the soul of beaming Mediterranean cordiality. But this morning his ruddy, genial complexion had turned pasty; the bright Latin eyes of last night were bloodshot and lifeless; the mountainous body which only twelve hours before might have put you in mind of a glowing and inexhaustible marine Bacchus was now flaccid and tired, uneasily foretasting decay.

10

'What do you want?' asked the Captain ungraciously, the smell of wine wafting about him as he came.

Banner, privately determining that he would have his revenge by means of the typewriter, explained. And when the truth finally sunk in Captain Gigi immediately looked as near to genial as he was able and belatedly offered his hand.

'Glass of wine,' he said, a statement more than an invitation and stumbled off to the bar behind the restaurant, returning with a litre flask of red and two glasses. His first drink went down in one; it was rather like watching a whale downing the contents of a champagne glass.

'What does it feel like, Captain, today—two years afterwards?'

Captain Gigi scratched his right buttock meditatively and prepared for speech.

As the interview went forward a strange phenomenon became noticeable. What with the wine and the adrenalin shot of publicity, life slowly filtered back into the vast expanses of Captain Gigi. And by the time it was over he was his evening self again, glowing with cordiality.

'You're quite sure there's nothing more you'd like to know?' he asked with the air of a girl facing imminent departure from her lover.

'Quite sure, thank you,' said Banner.

'If anything comes to mind, don't hesitate to get in touch.'

'I certainly will.'

'Well, in that case I suppose I'd better be getting off to my boat.'

If Captain Gigi's commission was spurious, he did at least have a boat. It was a one-time fishing boat called the *Lucrezia Borgia* and it looked as though it were in imminent peril of capsizing from the sheer weight of brightly coloured bunting with which it was decorated. He sailed this along the beach to pick up customers for what was euphemistically known as a fishing trip. He stopped at various points to issue loud-speaker invitations in Italian and then in his own highly individual English, French and German. At last when the boat was loaded to a point where the gunwales were practically underwater he

11

took her out from the shore, but not very far. When he got up to the lighthouse he headed her into the river Sile, chugged inland for five minutes and then turned back and repeated the journey in reverse. The fishing got overlooked on the way, but to make up for this the children on board were each presented with one rather dusty seashell from a plastic bag which Captain Gigi kept under his seat.

So now the Captain went to the *Lucrezia Borgia* and Banner to his car. He sat there in thought for a minute before switching on the engine. It was a curious thing but Captain Gigi had given him a distinct impression that the Free Jesolo Movement was a thing not only of the past, but of the present.

The second person who unwittingly had a line on to the unusual events that were preparing themselves in Jesolo was a photographer . . .

Benito Mussolini's life had been understandably much influenced by his name. This had been imposed on him by a father of obstinate and fervent right wing views who had flatly refused all suggestions that he should change the surname and then went on to compound the offence by giving his unhappy son the late dictator's Christian name as well.

For the first twenty years of his life this had brought nothing but misery to the young Benito. And then, just when he was on the point of having the name changed, he set up in business as a photographer and quickly began to realise that there were advantages to everything, even to being called Benito Mussolini. For people liked having their pictures taken by someone of that name; it lent a sort of arcane mystique to the business of photography. So instead of changing his name, Benito had it written in large letters over the front of his shop in Via Verdi.

This shop he ran with just one partner: a monkey named Desdemona who he found in every way preferable to human company. During the season the two of them would go out in the evening about their own stretch of Jesolo, and in the streets, bars, restaurants and *pizzerie*, Desdemona, glamorously dressed in scarlet uniform and cap, was placed in people's arms. Benito

12

would then snap the pair of them together, retrieve Desdemona and give the customer a ticket for picking up the photograph.

Photography, he found, was fairly rewarding and, as he also had quick and keen eyes, it served as a useful adjunct to his other, less openly avowable activities.

It was his involvement with these other activities which made him feel, illogically perhaps, offended when, a fortnight previously, his shop had been broken into; it was like being betrayed by colleagues. But Benito kept no money in the shop so the thief or thieves had got away with nothing more than several envelopes of negatives.

The point that had been worrying him ever since was why.

It occasionally happened that he snapped people who, for various reasons, didn't want to be snapped, and it seemed likely that something of the kind was behind the burglary of his shop. And it must have been something fairly serious to induce somebody to such extreme measures. Then again, why were so many negatives taken?

These were Benito's thoughts as he went, somewhat reluctantly, to the police station in Jesolo for his third interview with the policeman in charge of the investigation.

'Nothing more occurred to you about the subject of the pictures?' asked the detective named Roberti who was young, freckled and eager.

That's the third time we've been into that, thought Benito; this Roberti would be hard put to it to detect a black olive on a pizza. And maybe that was as well, too. Aloud he said, 'I know more or less where they were taken, but not of who.'

'Let's go through the list of all the places you think they were taken in . . .'

This was all the waste of time he'd known it was going to be; and Desdemona would be getting fretful back in the shop with the *Vengo Subito* notice stuck up on the door. Obviously Roberti, too, suspected that somebody had been in some way compromised by the Mussolini camera.

'But why were so *many* negatives taken?' asked Benito when he got the chance. 'One should have been enough—I never take more than one of the same person.'

13

'If they'd taken only one, it's just possible you might have been able to pin-point *which* one. But with a large number missing, that's obviously quite impossible.'

And that, thought Benito, was infuriatingly true.

Commissario Achille Peroni could already feel his warm, Neapolitan blood turn chill in anticipation of the clammy, fog-bound Venetian winter. Besides, for someone who liked his crime passionate and bubbling, being a policeman in Venice was like being an attendant in a museum and, what was more, a museum that was likely to crumble about your ears at any minute.

True, he had been involved in one murder investigation there, but when that had been concluded he had gone back to the routine patrolling of the museum. He had also been involved in one love affair which had sprung from the murder and given Peroni and the girl a brief period of idyllic happiness. But as often happens when happiness is so intense, it could not last, and that constituted yet another reason for his wanting to leave Venice, for its dark and narrow *calles* were haunted with the ghost of their love which even the swarming of a million tourists could not exorcise.

There was a pile of papers on the desk in Peroni's office and he now began to look through them perfunctorily. Just as he had imagined. A car radio stolen from Piazzale Roma. The proprietor of a *pensione* complaining about persistent late night rowdyism in the neighbourhood. A pensioner who claimed to have accidentally dropped her pension in the Grand Canal. The usual tran-tran of museum patrolling monotony.

And then quite unexpectedly something caught his eye. A missing persons report.

Kekzio Maisheilais. The name jumped at him from the paper and set him wondering whatever nationality or sex its owner might be. Then another, more familiar name leapt out of the report like a flying fish. Jesolo. So Kekzio Maisheilais had disappeared in Jesolo. An odd coincidence because Peroni's sister, Assunta, and her two children, Anna Maria and Stefano, were on holiday in Jesolo. He started to read the report systematically.

'Jesolo. 8.15, Tuesday, 17th September.' So it had only just been radioed through to Venice. 'Informant,' it went on, 'Skaialiu Sonaed.' A fitting companion for Kekzio Maisheilais, thought Peroni.

'Single,' said the report, clearing up at least one point, 'Aged 20. 17 Lnckhuuod Rod, Idainbiuajh, Scozia, Inghilterra.' Could Scotland be said to be in England? thought Peroni. And although his English could never be confounded with that of the Queen, he doubted whether there could be any such place as Lnckhuuod Rod, Idainbiuajh in either country.

From then on the going was easier as there were no further foreign words. Kekzio Maisheilais, it seemed, slept in a tent on the beach at Jesolo, though not in the official camping site. But for the last two nights he or she, according to Skaialiu Sonaed, had not come to his or her tent. This information was referred to the *Questura*—the police headquarters—of Venice, under the jurisdiction of which Jesolo came.

Peroni looked out of the office window. The Fondamenta San Lorenzo was deserted; it usually was, in fact, as few tourists ever go there except those who have lost their way to somewhere else. The church of San Lorenzo opposite looked more than ever as though it were on the point of imminent collapse. The canal below shifted sluggishly in its unspeakable bed. But the sun was shining brightly. It would be nice to see his sister and her family and spend a day by the sea.

15

Two

Shirley Conrad didn't trust the Italian police further than she could throw them. For one thing they didn't speak a word of English and, for another, when they did finally dig up somebody who could (in a manner of speaking) they started looking on her with the deepest mistrust as though, far from presenting herself voluntarily, she had been brought in on a charge of heaven only knew what monstrous crime.

And then the taking down of the report! Honestly, you'd think they'd never written out a report before in their lives! Everything had to be spelled out half a dozen times, and they kept on asking the same questions over and over again. And when it was finally done they told her to wait while they radioed it through to Venice, if you please! They'd never have got away with that at home.

Then after half an hour a man had come to say that a commissionaire or something was coming over from Venice and would she please wait until he arrived. Holy Harry what a police force! And then at last the same man as before came back and said would she step into the office as the commissionaire had arrived.

And as soon as she set foot in the office she decided she didn't trust the commissionaire either. Too good-looking by far with black eyes and black hair and what they called an olive-coloured complexion. And for Heaven's sake, what a tie for a policeman to wear!

Then he disconcerted her a bit by smiling with very white teeth and holding out his hand. She took it awkwardly and gave it back as quickly as she could. Why did these Italians always have to be shaking hands?

'You are Skaialiu Sonaed?' he said. The first two words were

16

just about recognisable English, but what in blue blazes did the rest mean?

'What's that?' she said.

'Skaialiu Sonaed,' he said. 'This is you?'

'It most sairtainly is not.'

At this he showed her a piece of paper on the desk in front of him, pointing at the name.

'Och, that's the young man that was taking it all down!' she said. 'I could see he didn't understand above a tenth of what I was saying to him! You don't have proper letters in your alphabet so he got them all muddled up. My name's Shirley Conrad.'

'Ah!' he said, looking enormously gratified as though her perspicacity had cleared up everything. 'Now,' he went on, 'I understand that this Kekzio Maisheilais is disappeared from a tent on the sand. Your boy-friend perhaps?'

Trust them to think of that straight away! 'No' she said. 'In fact, she's not a boy at all, she's a gairl. And her name's not Kekzio whatever-you-said either. It's Kehzia Michaelis.'

'Ah!' he said again, causing her a curious sensation in the region of her stomach. 'And this Kehzia is also English?'

'I'm not English—I'm Scots! And Kehzia is American.'

'You know her address in America?'

'No. In fact, I know very little about her altogether. I only met her for the fairst time a few days ago.'

'She is on holiday at Jesolo?'

'No. That much I can tell you. She sings in a sort of bar place called the Dolce Vita.'

'Have you asked for information about her there?'

'I have. I went in there last night. But they said they knew nothing about her.'

'But you did not come to the police yesterday?'

'Well, no. One night—I thought she might perhaps have stayed with somebody.' Infuriatingly, Shirley could feel herself blushing as she said it. 'But two nights is different. She wouldn't have left her tent unattended for that long.'

'You also sleep in a tent on the sand?'

'I do.'

17

'Why do you not go to the official camping?' He pronounced it with the emphasis on the last syllable which came out as peeng.

'You wouldn't ask that if you tried to go there!' she said. 'The prices are downright scandalous!'

'But is it secure for two young ladies to sleep alone on the sand?'

'I can look after myself!'

'And Kehzia—can she also look after herself?'

'She's mebbe more lightweight that I am, but I think she can. She's been hitch-hiking her way about in more than a dozen other countries.'

'This Kehzia,' he said after a pause, 'she is a friend of yours?'

'I told you, I've only known her for a few days.'

'It is enough a few minutes that people are friends. May be a few seconds.'

She looked at him quickly. It was almost as though he sensed the adoration she had felt for Kehzia since the first moment they had met; an adoration so overwhelming she was more than half ashamed of it.

'We were friends,' she admitted guardedly.

'I think,' he said getting up, 'we go to see the tent. You come with me in the police car,' he went on, adding as an afterthought, 'I think we shall use the siren.'

This commissionaire, Shirley thought, was certainly unexpected and perhaps quite nice, though she still wouldn't trust him, of course. Give her a good Scottish bobbie any day of the week.

This girl with stringy fair hair, red hands and a somewhat overpronounced bottom was a bit of a novelty for Peroni. She had greeted him with downright hostility, and even now, with the siren thrown in for good measure as well, she maintained a certain guarded wariness. Anything less from a young female than total surrender in sixty seconds left Peroni feeling like a chess master defeated by somebody who's only just discovered the difference between a pawn and a bishop.

Moreover the effort of speaking English had left him feeling a

18

bit shaky. Some years before he had had a six months' special posting to New Scotland Yard during which he had become a passionate Anglophile and acquired a somewhat tousled knowledge of the language, but although he still sometimes spoke it for the private entertainment of friends and relatives, the passing of time had made it an ever greater effort.

The car drew up on a sand-swept road leading to a bay and a low stone building with benches and tables outside. Just beyond this was the mouth of the river Sile where it flowed into the sea, and on the other side of the river, where its bank formed a headland, stood a towering, striped lighthouse. A fishing boat, smothered in bunting and holiday-makers, chugged laboriously into the Sile with an abundant man in naval uniform at the steering wheel.

'Down here,' said the girl called Shirley Conrad.

They went from the road onto the beach and started to walk across the sand. A group of American servicemen in swimming trunks were sitting in a circle playing cards, drinking beer from cans and smoking. Two large negroes, also in swimming trunks, were playing with a Frisbee, throwing it backwards and forwards between them over an almost incredible distance and leaping high to pluck it out of the air with a single finger.

Kehzia's tent was a dark brown, Canadian ridge type and Peroni had to wriggle into it snake-fashion so that the sand got up his sleeves and into his shoes.

It was hot inside with the strong, unmistakable smell that all tents have. It was also untidy. A sleeping bag was bundled up at the farther end with jeans, shirts and gym-shoes; there was also a plastic bag with toilet articles.

For a moment Peroni thought that was the sum of it, then feeling under the sleeping bag he found an old knapsack which seemed to be empty, but pulping it carefully Peroni found something flat and hard in one of its pockets. He opened the pocket and pulled out a dark blue document with an eagle on the cover. A U.S. passport. He opened it and suddenly the image of a girl made a tiger spring at his eyes.

The photograph had the slightly unreal air of all passport photographs, yet it told him clearly that he was meeting

19

someone who was going to upset his entire life. She was
beautiful with a grave, dark, and at the same time, flashing
beauty. Her hair was black and her eyes, frustratingly en-
igmatic, were almost certainly black, too. Something about her
put Peroni in mind of pictures he had seen of Israeli girl fighters,
their utter femininity highlighted and enhanced by their
cumbersome uniforms; and the association made him realise
that she was probably Jewish.

'Have you found something?'

The voice of the girl with the large bottom made him wonder
how long he had been crouched there staring at the little square
photograph.

'Her passport,' he said.

Peroni glanced quickly through the basic facts concerning
Kehzia and learned that she had been born twenty-five years
before at Providence, Rhode Island.

The tent had nothing more to say about its owner and Peroni
wriggled out of it backwards thoughtfully. He questioned the
other people camping nearby, but found that most of them had
only arrived the previous night. Only two young Americans
said they knew her by sight and that they had last seen her
walking off down the beach two mornings before. Their
expressions as they talked of her confirmed the opinion which
had forced itself on Peroni as he studied the photograph.

'What are you going to do now?' asked Shirley Conrad.

Peroni wondered whether the Scottish police allowed themselves to be so hectored. Aloud he merely said, 'I'm going to
have this photograph blown up and distributed. Then I'm going
to pay a visit to the Dolce Vita.'

Three

The Dolce Vita was not hard to find. It was down towards the end of Jesolo village main street opposite a cinema devoted entirely to pornography.

'*Pizza*,' Peroni read outside, '*English Breackfast. Tea Like Mother Makes It—No Bags. Ice's Cream—Own Production.*'

Peroni went beneath the awning outside and into a deserted restaurant. At the other end of this were two doors inside one of which he could see a bar counter. He went through the door and stopped in astonishment.

It was as though he had walked back in time at least fifty years. An instant before he had been in the Jesolo of *Tea Like Mother Makes It*; now he was back in the old Jesolo village before the lido has been strung like a collection of ugly and gaudy pearls upon the string of the beach. It was a shock that there ever had been an old Jesolo at all.

He was in fact in what had once been a village *osteria*, rough, smoky with a stone floor and what were evidently the original wooden chairs and tables. There was even the old crucifix on the wall behind the bar. Beneath this crucifix, however, was a specimen of modern Jesolo, a cocky young waiter probably not yet out of his teens. He was looking at the sports pages of a newspaper and didn't seem eager to be distracted from them.

'*Questura*,' said Peroni.

At least that took his mind off football. 'Captain Gigi's out,' he said.

'And who,' said Peroni, 'is Captain Gigi?'

'The boss,' said the waiter, looking baffled.

'Never mind,' said Peroni equably, 'we can do without him. I daresay you can be just as helpful.' He paused and then said 'Kehzia Michaelis,' watching lust flash like slow lightning in the waiter's eyes. 'When did you last see her?'

'The night before last.'

'She sang here as usual then?'

'That's right.'

'What happened when she didn't turn up last night?'

'Nothing special. People come and go easily at the seaside.'

'Did somebody take her place?'

'No need. The rest of the programme went on as usual with Ornella.'

'Ornella?'

'She's the girl who regularly sings with the orchestra. Signorina Kehzia was a sort of extra with a spot of her own.'

'What time did she leave on Saturday night?'

'Same as always—about midnight.'

'Alone?'

'Yes.'

'On foot?'

'Yes, but she must have caught a bus. One or two evenings I've seen her at the bus stop.'

'Did you speak to her the evening before last?'

'Just "*Buona sera, Signorina*".'

In a flash of empathy, Peroni felt the young waiter's helpless frustration as he longed for the beautiful American girl and yet was able to say no more than "*Buona sera, Signorina*" to her.

'Did you notice anything at all unusual about her manner?'

The waiter frowned. 'Yes,' he said, almost surprised at himself, 'I think I did. She's been sort of funny lately. As though she was worried about something.'

'Men friends?'

'I've seen her with a couple.' A painful subject. Then something seemed to occur to the waiter and he looked carefully through the door before speaking. 'Captain Gigi was after her,' he said.

'Was he indeed?'

Suddenly the waiter's attention sharpened at something behind Peroni. 'That's Maurizio,' he said. 'He directs the orchestra. He might be able to tell you something more about her. Maurizio!' he called.

22

'Yes?' They were joined by a small, plump, rosy man with gold-rimmed spectacles, an alarmingly designed purple shirt and dimpled knees showing beneath Bermuda shorts.

'This gentleman—' began the waiter and then found himself cut short.

'*Questura*,' snapped Peroni, wondering why he had suddenly transformed himself into a brusque police functionary, 'I'm enquiring about the whereabouts of Kehzia Michaelis.'

'Oh,' said Maurizio sounding relieved, 'I'm sure there's nothing to enquire about *there*!'

'Why not?'

'People like that come and go *all* the time. She probably just found a new man and went off with him. *Do* let me get you a drink, Commissario.'

'No thank you,' said Peroni. He now understood his sudden transformation. Maurizio was a *finocchio*, and moreover a *finocchio* with his eye on Peroni.

'Why do you think she went off with a man?' he asked.

'She's the *type*,' said Maurizio contemptuously, 'I don't know *why* Gigi keeps her.'

In view of what the waiter had just said Peroni thought he had a shrewd idea of the answer to that, but he merely said, 'Isn't she a good singer?'

'Oh, I don't know about *good*,' said Maurizio, edging a little nearer to Peroni, 'She was too *intellectual* for a place like this. She wrote her own songs—all about silver fish and golden apples and bitter wine and unborn children—*you* know the sort of thing, Commissario. *Not* suitable for package deal holiday-makers.'

'Have you ever seen her about with any particular man?' asked Peroni, shifting away from Maurizio.

'Yes, there is one,' said Maurizio. 'Good-looking,' he added with the tone of a connoisseur.

'Can you describe him?'

'Tall, slim,' said Maurizio frowning in concentration, 'in his early forties perhaps, but very young looking. Like a Greek *god*.'

'That's right,' said the waiter who had been leaning on the

counter following the exchanges, 'I've seen him. He'd sit at a table by himself drinking Pernod and watching her while she sang.'

'Always Pernod?' asked Peroni curiously.

'Always Pernod,' said the waiter, 'and a lot of it.'

'An Italian?'

'Yes.'

'On holiday?'

'No,' said the waiter decidedly, 'not the type for Jesolo— Costa Azzurra more like or Sardinia.'

'That's right,' said Maurizio, piqued that the waiter had gained the ascendant in the conversation, 'Rich by the look of him. *Lovely* clothes!'

'Any idea where he comes from?'

'Judging by the look of him,' said the waiter, 'and the fact that he could be here so often, I should say he must live in Venice.'

This waiter is bright, thought Peroni. 'Any chance of a photograph of Signorina Kehzia?' he asked.

'As a matter of fact there *is*,' squeaked Maurizio, delighted to beat the waiter to it this time. 'There's one that Gigi had for sticking up outside. I'll go and get it at *once*.'

He wiggled coquettishly away and was back a minute later with a large photograph which he handed, simpering, to Peroni.

It was immediately evident that this photograph would be of far more practical value than the passport head and shoulders. It also drew him several strides further in emotionally.

It was a large glossy, a little faded by the sun, but an eminently sharp portrait of Kehzia. Her head was turned towards the camera and her dark eyes seemed to be looking for somebody. Her lips were parted slightly and Peroni had the wild sensation that, if only he could catch it, she was saying something that was meant for him.

Assunta dalla Vedova lifted the lid of the small pan and noted that the clams were sizzling nicely in the oil along with the skinned tomatoes and the garlic. She looked at her watch. Twenty-five to one. It was time the children came in from the beach.

24

She went out onto the balcony to look for them. Yes, that was Stefano sitting in the shade of an umbrella poring over a chess problem. And that black head bobbing some way out in the dazzling blue and silver water was Anna Maria.

'*Bambini*!' she shouted. 'Stefano! Anna Maria! Lunch!'

The beach at this hour echoed with the seagull cries of mothers calling their broods in to lunch from the balconies which overlooked the beach. 'Massimo!' you could hear, 'Lucia! Marco! Isabella!' And usually the cries persisted for some while, for half the children didn't hear and the other half pretended not to. But after Assunta had been at it for a couple of minutes Stefano looked up like one coming out of a dream and waved owlish acquiescence.

She went back into the flat and put the water on for the spaghetti. Then the doorbell rang and she went to answer it. It was her brother, totally unexpected as usual.

'*Ciao*, Assunta.'

'*Ciao*, Achille. Whatever are you doing in Jesolo?'

'I've got a job here,' he said vaguely.

There was still a strong bond of affection between Peroni and his sister. In childhood they had been *scugnizzi* or gutter kids in Naples, but with the years respectability had taken them along separate paths. She had married a rolling, jolly northerner, an architect named Giorgio dalla Vedova, and produced two children. He had become a policeman and, characteristically she supposed, a famous policeman, labelled by the media with the ridiculous epithet of "the Rudolph Valentino of the Italian police". The nickname always made her furious; it gave such a blatantly false impression of her doubt-beset, conceited and fallible brother. He was, she had to admit, tolerably good-looking and more easily taken in by unsuitable women than most men, but there the resemblance ended.

She looked at him more sharply. There was something about his expression which suggested that he was in the process of being taken in by an unsuitable woman at the moment. Not for the first time she decided that she must set about finding a suitable one for him to marry.

'*Spaghetti alle vongole*?' he asked sniffing. She nodded. 'Good,' he said. 'Where are the children?'

'They're on their way up now.'

'How's Giorgio?' Assunta's husband had remained behind in Verona, where they lived, working.

'He's fine,' she said. 'He telephoned last night. He'll be over for the weekend.'

At this there was a sudden staccato clattering of clog-sandals outside followed by an insistent, non-stop peal of the doorbell, and when Assunta had opened the door Stefano, aged eleven, and Anna Maria, aged fifteen, burst into the flat with towels flying like banners at a mediaeval tournament.

'*Ciao*, Uncle Achille!' they shouted delightedly when they saw him.

'Whatever brings you to Jesolo?' asked Anna Maria.

'Don't tell them, Achille,' said Assunta quickly. 'Let them wash their hands first and get ready to come to table.'

More or less cheerfully they accepted this ruling and clattered off to get ready.

'Well?' demanded Stefano when they were finally seated and Assunta was ladelling the steaming coils of pasta onto their plates.

'Nothing all that special,' said Peroni. 'A girl is missing.'

There's one at least who won't be able to make a fool of him, thought Assunta. Unless, of course, he finds her.

'Foul play suspected?' enquired Anna Maria.

'I don't think so,' said Peroni. 'I hope not.'

Assunta wondered why there should be a hint of anxiety in her brother's tone.

'You don't know this girl by any chance, Achille?' she asked.

'No, no—I've never set eyes on her.'

Well, that's something to be thankful for, thought Assunta.

'What do you know about her, Uncle Achille?' asked Anna Maria.

'Well, she's American,' said Peroni, 'Named Kehzia Michaelis—'

'What an extraordinary name,' said Assunta disapprovingly.

'And she sang at a place called the Dolce Vita in Jesolo village. She's apparently been hitch-hiking her way about the world—'

26

'Foot-loose!'

'Where did she live in Jesolo?' asked Stefano.

'She had a tent up at the end of the beach by the lighthouse.'

'Alone?'

'Apparently.'

In her more logical moments Assunta was keenly aware of the disparity between her own youthful conduct in Naples and her present highly moral standards. She knew quite well that in disapproving of what she imagined was Kehzia Michaelis's way of life she was condemning her own past. But that didn't stop her from giving vent to the exasperation which everything she heard about the girl seemed to arouse in her.

'A girl like that,' she said, 'can expect anything she gets.'

She felt a twinge of guilt as she said it, but not even remotely did she expect her brother's reaction.

To the consternation of the family, Achille Peroni slammed his spaghetti-laden fork down onto his plate and left the flat without a word.

Four

There had been perplexity in ministerial circles when Perez had first applied to join the police. For official physical qualifications state that candidates should have no physical handicaps or impediments. And what worried senior functionaries in Rome was that Perez was an albino. Not a total albino, but nevertheless recognisably an albino.

Some functionaries held that this disqualified him; others argued that albinoism was neither a handicap nor an impediment. Finally the case went to the minister who ruled for the second group, and Perez was recruited.

Since then he had been occupied with many jobs, but few that he considered more of a waste of time than the one he was on at the moment. He was hawking the photograph of a girl named Michaelis about Jesolo, and this he held to be a waste of time because the girl had been missing for less than forty-eight hours and when good-looking girls like that were missing for anything less than a week at the minimum, Perez did not believe the police should be bothered.

However, Perez was also a conscientious policeman and moreover, although a northerner with all the northerner's habitual distrust of the south, he had a stirring of respect for Commissario Peroni from whom the order had come, and so he had put his own judgement temporarily aside and taken the photograph about Jesolo like an eccentric commercial traveller.

So far without results. He had been into several dozen establishments of various natures only to meet with negatives accompanied by displays of greater or lesser interest in the photograph according to age or sex.

Now he was coming into Piazza Trento. On one side of the piazza was a large, concrete church with broad steps leading up

28

to it. What Perez imagined he knew of the Michaelis girl led him
to decide that a church was not the place to find traces of her.

On another side of the piazza was a bar and, reckoning that a
more likely bet, he went in and ordered himself a coffee, taking
an albino count automatically as he did so. Perez had first
started taking albino counts when he was at school: they were a
numerical assessment, ranging from zero to ten, of people's
reactions to his albinoism. This time he got a seven from the
proprietor, a tall, thin man with rodent features and quick eyes.

'*Questura*,' he said when the coffee was placed before him,
getting a nine-plus count on that one. 'Have you ever seen this
girl around?'

The quick eyes razored onto the photograph. 'Yes,' he said,
'I've seen her a couple of times.'

'In here?'

'No,' said the man, gesturing with his chin, 'over there.
Going into that house by the church. The presbytery.'

Peroni bitterly regretted his conduct at his sister's. Largely
because a senior police officer just does not behave like a stupid
adolescent over a girl of whom he has seen no more than the
photograph. Partly also because *spaghetti alle vongole* was one
of his favourite dishes. And so regret ploughed him; but it was
quickly replaced by excitement when Perez told him of the
unusual lead he had uncovered and he went immediately to
Piazza Trento.

Presbyteries, he thought, as he waited outside the front door,
can be as unexpectedly idiosyncratic as the priests who live in
them. Where he came from himself they tended to be ancient
with flaking remains of a long since repented worldly glory
which had shone in the days when the church in the south had
had something at any rate in common with the Mafia. There
were your humble presbyteries which nestle deferentially
beneath the campanile. And your businesslike ones with several
doorbells and a speaker which quacks at you when you ring
them, and various notice boards telling you about a pilgrimage
to Lourdes, a course for engaged couples, the times of masses

and the moral ratings of the various films showing at local cinemas.

This presbytery was like none of these. It was a typical product of Jesolo: characterless and functional.

The door was opened by a short, stocky, powerful looking man somewhere in his fifties wearing an immaculately ironed overall. He had close-cropped hair, a taurine neck and sharp black eyes which looked at Peroni suspiciously.

'Yes?' said the man in a tone that suggested "No".

'I should like to speak to Don Zaccaria,' said Peroni who had learned the priest's name from Perez.

'He's busy.'

'When could I find him?' Peroni was suddenly deceptively genial.

'What's your business?' The man's tone indicated that it was just a question of determining which particular detergent Peroni was hawking.

'Can I help you?'

The phrase was just in time to prevent Peroni chopping down the man with a staccato '*Questura*' and it was accompanied by the speaker, a tall man, severely dressed in a cassock with a face of horse-like melancholy and sagging eyes. Most priests, Peroni knew, could be divided into pre-and post-Vatican II in their ways of regarding life; a glance was enough to label this one as pre.

'Don Zaccaria?' Peroni asked.

The priest inclined his head in penitential assent.

'I should like to speak to you for a moment.'

'Please come in.'

Peroni stepped past the overalled man who looked at him in mute hostility. He found himself in a tiny, dark hallway which looked as though it had been brought to an almost supernatural state of neatness and high polish by a process of the harshest asceticism.

'In here,' said Don Zaccaria and led Peroni into a study which had obviously been subjected to the same penitential rigours as the hall. All the objects in the room seemed to know their places to the nearest millimetre. Some heavy volumes stood in precise file behind the glass front of a bookcase like members of some military-monastic order. Even the saints whose pictures hung upon the walls seemed to be standing to attention.

'You must excuse Bo,' said Don Zaccaria after closing the door.

'Bo?' said Peroni, baffled.

'My sacristan—Teodorico Bo. He is an excellent man, most attentive to his duties and deeply pious, but he tends to be difficult with strangers. Please be seated. What can I do for you?'

'I'm from the *Questura*,' said Peroni who found himself talking in the whispering, intimate tone of one in the confessional, though this may have been partly due to the fact that his instinct told him that Bo was listening behind the door.

If Don Zaccaria was put out by the news that Peroni was from the *Questura* he didn't show it; he merely raised his bushy eyebrows a fraction in a mute but polite "Oh, yes?"

'I'm making enquiries about this girl,' said Peroni showing the photograph.

This time there was a reaction. Don Zaccaria's equine features tensed and Peroni felt waves of emotion emanating from him.

'What has she done?'

It sounded as though he were expecting her to have done something.

'What do you think she might have done?' countered Peroni without losing the intimate confessional tone.

'I think nothing. I just presumed that if the police are making enquiries about a young woman she must have done something.'

He was guarded now and Peroni realised with irritation that the moment when he could have been taken by surprise had passed.

'She'd been coming here to see you?'

Don Zaccaria's long head moved in cautious assent.

'For long?'

'Only about two weeks.'

31

'How many times did she come in all?'

'Four.'

'What did she come about?'

There was a long dry pause, and Peroni thought he could detect a stir of movement behind the door; he contemplated tip-toeing across and pulling it suddenly open, but then thought how stupid he would have looked if Bo wasn't there.

'I'm afraid I cannot tell you that.' Great deliberation.

'The secret of the confessional?'

'Call it that.'

'She's a Catholic then?'

A pause. 'No.'

'Then the confessional secrecy can't be binding.'

'Other confidences may be made to a priest which demand his silence as much as those made in the confessional.'

'Is this canonically established?'

'Yes.'

'Even if the information were necessary for a police investigation?'

'I would have to have authorisation from the Cardinal Patriarch of Venice before revealing the motive for her visits.'

The gutter kid inside Peroni whistled irreverently. Big potatoes! Always assuming it was true, of course. The priest might perfectly well have been making it all up to cover up something altogether more mundane. Like an affair with Kehzia. Peroni winced at the thought.

'Would you consider asking the Cardinal Patriarch for authorisation?'

'I would have to have considerable motivation.'

Peroni paused for a second, calculating his shot. 'The girl's disappeared,' he said.

Again the almost tangible waves of a strong but undefinable emotion.

'When was this?'

'She hasn't been seen since the night before last.'

'One day.'

'And two nights,' Peroni reminded the priest who, irritatingly, seemed reassured by the shortness of the period.

'A girl of that age wandering about the world might well take it into her head to go off for a day or two.'

Oh, the infuriatingly calm wisdom of mother church!

'When did you last see her?'

'Last Thursday.'

Five days before. 'There was nothing in her manner then that gave you any indication she might be going off?'

Don Zaccaria seemed to ponder this. 'I couldn't always tell what was going on in her mind,' he said at length.

'When were you expecting to see her again?'

'Some time this week.'

Peroni got up. When a priest waved a Cardinal Patriarch at you, however discreetly, you were up against a fairly considerable obstacle. Whatever motives Kehzia may have had for visiting Don Zaccaria, Peroni was not going to be made a party to them for the present at any rate.

The two men shook hands without cordiality and Don Zaccaria opened the study door. Peroni emerged, as though from the confessional, and saw Bo polishing a small table which was already resplendent with his attentions. The sacristan looked at him with the same implacable dislike and Peroni pretended not to notice.

'You'll get in touch with us immediately if you hear anything of her?'

'Naturally.'

Don Zaccaria held open the front door and Peroni stepped out from the hushed, dark presbytery into the September sun. Out in the Piazza again he looked back at the trim, characterless little presbytery with its horse-like master and his hostile sacristan who listened at doors.

They had secrets, those two, thought Peroni. And a sudden intuition told him it was not going to be easy to uncover them.

In the meantime two people needed seeing: Captain Gigi and the Pernod drinker. And first of all the identity of the Pernod drinker would somehow have to be discovered.

33

Five

Etymologically speaking, the name Barba Gianni is something of a jungle. *Barba* in Italian means beard, but in archaic use and Venetian dialect it means uncle. Gianni is a diminutive of Giovanni and can roughly be translated Johnnie. Put the two together and you think you've got Uncle Johnnie, but the jungle is not finished, for a Gianni preceded by a *barba* also means both a type of owl and a fool. Both of these senses could be and had been attached to the present Barba Gianni. He was as predatory as the owl and few men in Italy could have deserved the second application of the words more richly to judge by appearances.

But only by appearances. For few men could have deserved it less to judge by intelligence.

Barba Gianni looked the perfect fool. What remained to him of hair stuck up about his head in unruly spikes; his mouth as often as not hung open, and if a scarecrow swapped clothes with him, it would undoubtedly have got the better of the bargain.

But until his retirement some five years previously Barba Gianni had been one of the shrewdest policemen in Europe who went as unerringly for the truth as a pig for truffles. Since his retirement he had spent practically his entire waking existence in an *osteria* known as the Half Moon where he consumed an incalculable number of what in Venetian dialect are known as shades of wine.

He liked the Half Moon because it was unfrequented by tourists, down at heel, dark and noisy, and he was able to sit in a corner with his wine in front of him, smoking a gnarled Tuscan cigar and creating and solving and re-creating endlessly in his mind the most abstruse and labyrinthine problems with an odd

34

mixture of pure mathematics and intuition.

He was engaged in doing this when he realised that somebody was standing beside him. He looked up and was uncertain for an instant whether it was a real person or one of the characters from his problems who did occasionally appear to materialise. This uncertainty was prolonged by the fact that he knew the face, but not its owner.

Then, like the solution of a too easy problem, the answer came to him. It was Achille Peroni, the Neapolitan detective. If only half of what he had heard about Peroni was true, then the Neapolitan was the only man in the peninsula whose capacities were even remotely comparable to his own.

'Peroni,' he said, stating a fact. 'Barba Gianni,' he said, stating another. 'This is a meeting of legends. Sit down.'

'Let me get some more wine to celebrate the meeting,' said Peroni and went to the counter to order it.

As he waited Barba Gianni tried to work out why Peroni had come. A purely social visit or an act of homage, no; working policemen always put such occasions off till tomorrow. Help of some sort then. But one legend would not permit itself to ask help of another. Unless. There could be nothing demeaning in calling upon Barba Gianni's purely Venetian knowledge which Peroni could not be expected to share. He wanted to know something about Venice then. A particular place? No, for that sort of information is all stored up in archives at the *Questura*. An event? No, for the same reason. A person then. But once again not a person whose identity Peroni already knew, for then the resources of the *Questura* would again be sufficient for him. Therefore it must be somebody of whom Peroni only had a description which he now wanted to link up with an identity.

Peroni returned with a litre of wine and poured out for them both.

'Describe him,' said Barba Gianni, 'this Venetian you want me to identify.'

For a split second Peroni looked disconcerted—a chess master put into unexpected check—but then he had it worked out and smiled an impudent Neapolitan smile of pure appreciation. This one is good, thought Barba Gianni.

35

'It's a man,' said Peroni, 'a rich man. Tall and expensively dressed. In his early forties and with the look of a Greek god, as somebody put it. And a heavy Pernod drinker. That's all I have.'

'Too easy,' said Barba Gianni with disappointment, swallowing a shade of wine in one, 'Fabrizio de Sanctis. If you're sure it's a Venetian you want, it can't be anyone else.'

'You've saved me a lot of time,' said Peroni.

Barba Gianni shrugged. 'As I say, it was too easy. It's an old Venetian family. Too old. They've got a palace just off Campo SS Giovanni e Paolo.'

'It's all I need,' said Peroni, 'I'm grateful.'

'Don't mention it, but next time try and bring me something more difficult.'

Barba Gianni considered calling Peroni back as he was going, to ask him what his interest was in de Sanctis, but then he decided to deduce it for himself. It would make an entertaining problem.

The de Sanctis palace was an island in the heart of Venice. You reached it by crossing a little bridge which humped over one of the surrounding canals taking you to a broad strip of paving before the classically elegant three-storied façade of the palace with its marble balconies and intricately carved pillared windows.

Peroni crossed the bridge admiring the sleek motor boats moored to the dark blue and golden poles. Then he climbed the broad steps and passed between columns to the front door. As he rang it, he noticed the expensive gleam of the bell.

The door was opened by a slim, good-looking young man with a mass of tousled gold hair, very much a student, wearing jeans, t-shirt and gym-shoes. 'Can I help you?' he said.

'*Questura*,' said Peroni and registered an almost imperceptible flicker of alarm, though there was no telling whether it was the normal human reaction at finding a policeman on the front doorstep or whether there was some more specific motive for it. 'I'd like to speak to Signor de Sanctis.'

'That's me.'

Which didn't fit at all, thought Peroni; the young man was far too young for Maurizio's description of the Pernod drinker. 'Signor Fabrizio de Sanctis,' he specified.

'Oh, Papa.' The explanation was simple enough; for some reason Peroni hadn't been expecting grown-up children. 'I'm afraid he's out at the moment, but if you'd like to come in and wait I'm expecting him back at any minute.' De Sanctis junior, now completely at his ease, stood aside as he said this.

Peroni was expecting luxury, but even so he was taken aback by the inside of the palace. While everything that was old had been maintained, it was shored up and accompanied by very costly and discreet modernity. The marble floor of the large hall had been trod by Venetians who had been alive at the battle of Lepanto, but on it was a powder blue Persian carpet. The carved stonework of the wall facing the front door had been wrought by masons who could also have worked on the doge's palace, but hanging upon it in perfect harmony was a picture Peroni identified with awe.

It showed, in the foreground, a large bunch of bananas on a flat surface which seemed to have been deftly and just perceptibly wrenched out of the rectangular and, in the background, which stretched away absolutely flat to a distant sea, there stood two Greek statues staring ahead of them with dead, stone eyes.

It was a de Chirico.

'Won't you come in?'

The young man was holding open a door on the left of the hall, and as he went through it Peroni admired the same skilful blending of ancient and modern he had noticed in the hall. With a deepening of awe he noticed a second de Chirico, a Picasso and a Roualt.

'You know,' said the young man, having gestured for him to sit, 'I have the feeling I've seen you somewhere before.'

There was something unusually charming about him. Peroni glowed and allowed himself to be transformed into his own legend.

'*Questura?*' said the young man reflectively. He concentrated for a second, then flicked his fingers as the solution slotted into place. 'I have it,' he said. 'Commissario Achille Peroni! I've seen your photograph many times. Whatever has Papa done?'

Peroni felt this might be an opportunity for starting his enquiry; after all, de Sanctis junior might also have been involved with Kehzia.

'I'm only making enquiries about a missing person,' he said, producing the photograph. 'Have you ever seen this girl?'

The young man studied it with virile, but apparently quite detached, appreciation. 'No,' he said, 'I'd have remembered her if I had. But if she's one of Papa's girl-friends—' Peroni felt a sharp twinge of jealousy '—I wouldn't be very likely to have seen her. I'm at Ferrara most of the time. At university. Our social lives are quite separate.' At this point he broke off and cocked his head in a listening attitude. 'I think that's Papa now,' he said. 'Excuse me. I'll go and look.'

He went out, returning a few seconds later with a tall man who fitted Maurizio's description to perfection. Like his son, he showed no trace of discomfiture as he stepped towards Peroni with his hand outstretched.

'Commissario Peroni!' he said, 'Marco told me you were here. How delightful! I knew you'd been seconded to Venice, but never expected to have the pleasure of seeing you here. What can I do for you?'

'Before you start, Papa,' said Marco de Sanctis, 'I'll say goodbye. I'm off to Ferrara.' He shook hands politely with Peroni, said —'*Ciao*' to his father and then left them.

'Drink, Commissario?' said de Sanctis.

Peroni still felt the wine he had consumed with Barba Gianni, but he said he would like a whisky just the same. and then de Sanctis, when he had poured this, almost as though out of bravado, produced a bottle of Pernod, pouring himself a large measure and adding just enough water to obtain the cloudy effect.

As he raised the glass in a silent toast and drank, something about him made Peroni realise that it was by no means the first glass that day. This was intuition more than deduction, for nothing about de Sanctis showed he had been drinking.

'What can I do for you, Commissario?' he asked for the second time.

Peroni produced Kehzia's photograph again. 'Have you ever seen this girl?' he asked.

De Sanctis looked at it. 'Yes,' he said, 'I know her.' There was emotion there and, perhaps to hide it, he reached for something on a low, glass table beside him. It was a hand-shaker game, a tiny maze through which you had to steer a little silver ball, tipping it to avoid holes at the various junctions. He man-oeuvered it with remarkable deftness and speed along part of the course, then deliberately let the ball slip into one of the holes. 'Forgive me,' he said, 'I really ought to see a psychiatrist. I'm addicted to these gewgaws. Yes, I do know Kehzia. What's happened to her?'

(Don Zaccaria had asked "What has she done?" Now de Sanctis was asking "What's happened to her?" Did the questions reflect the speakers' attitudes to her, the one believing that she acted and the other that she was acted upon? Or did one of the questions reveal that the speaker of it *knew*?)

'Do you expect something to have happened to her?' asked Peroni.

'Your visit, Commissario.'

(Much the same answer, too, as Don Zaccaria had made.)

'When did you last see her?'

'About twelve days ago. She came to a small dinner party here.'

'And you've had no news of her since?'

'None.'

'You haven't been worried?'

'Kehzia's like quicksilver. And she goes her own way.'

'How long have you known her?'

'About four months.'

'How did you first meet her?'

Once again Peroni sensed strong emotion, and once again de Sanctis started the tiny ball off along the track and past a couple of holes before answering. 'Somebody mentioned that an American girl was singing her own, very original songs at the Dolce Vita in Jesolo. So I went to hear her. I liked what I heard

39

very much and I asked her if she would come and sing at a dinner party I was giving. This was difficult because she was engaged every evening at the Dolce Vita, so we finally agreed that a car should pick her up one evening after her final group of songs. The evening, when it came, was no small success.'

'What are her songs like?' asked Peroni.

De Sanctis flicked the silver ball along another couple of narrow corridors. 'Very simple. Veined with melancholy. And set to curiously—inescapable melodies.'

'And after that first dinner party?' went on Peroni.

'I asked her to one or two others. And sometimes during the day I've accompanied her on visits about the city. She has a passion for art, for antiquity. For the past.'

'For the past?' repeated Peroni, sensing emphasis in the phrase.

'Yes. It's as though if she only interrogates it scrupulously enough it will finally yield up a secret she is searching for.'

For some while now an unasked question had been throbbing like neuralgia in Peroni's head. He was afraid of the answer, but he had to ask for it.

'One last point. What is the nature of your relationship with Kehzia Michaelis?'

'We're friends.'

'No more than that?'

'What could there be more than that?'

De Sanctis guided the silver ball round the last seemingly unavoidable hole to the finish. Behind the ambiguity of the answer, Peroni sensed the same powerful emotion as before, and for all the satisfaction it had given him the question would have been better unasked. The flood-gates of jealousy were now fully open within him and there was nothing whatsoever he could do about it. He stood up to go.

'Just one thing,' said de Sanctis at the door. 'Why are you enquiring after Kehzia Michaelis?'

'She's disappeared,' said Peroni, watching carefully.

Something like muffled lightning flickered behind de Sanctis's eyes.

Six

The coloured lights swayed hypnotically backwards and forwards; waiters swooped and dipped among the tables juggling with extraordinary dexterity pizzas, spaghetti, steak and chips, fish and chips and all the other delicacies advertised in four languages outside, as well as flasks of wine and huge mugs of frothing beer; holiday-makers, mostly middle-aged Germans and English, perched on the benches calling and shouting to each other like the inhabitants of a monstrously overcrowded human rookery, while those of them who could squeeze onto the dance floor swayed self-consciously backwards and forwards clasping each other about the waist.

The evening's fun at the Dolce Vita was at its height.

Maurizio, his plump form nestling in a pair of flared white trousers and a crimson silk shirt, his gold spectacles glinting in the many-coloured lights, was enthusiastically directing the three-piece orchestra, announcing the various pieces and making coy gags in German and English and every so often picking up his concertina and squeezing sound out of it with theatrical tenderness.

This whole festive scene was dominated by Captain Gigi, belly and buttocks swelling like plump hillocks, as he made his regal passage among the tables, his round face glowing like the sun in a mediaeval manuscript, cradling a glass of wine in one fat hand and a cigarette in the other; here bestowing the largesse of a smile, there of a word; the undisputed master of the revels.

He made Peroni think of a circus clown he had once seen beneath whose paint-caked face with its enormous grin and glowing nose you could make out hardness, coldness and calculation.

Twice the Captain passed by Peroni's table, but he didn't see him. Captain Gigi didn't actually see anybody; he merely saw himself reflected in other people.

It was time to spear him. Peroni was on the point of standing up when the music stopped and Maurizio picked up the microphone which he fondled and brushed against his lips as he spoke.

'Signori e signore,' he said, 'Damen und herren, ladies and gentlemen—may I introduce for your attention and applause the delightful Signorina Ornella who will now sing for you!'

He held out his chubby, be-ringed hand in a wide gesture and a fair-haired girl in a green evening dress climbed onto the rostrum. Peroni momentarily postponed the spearing of Captain Gigi in order to see this girl who had been Kehzia's colleague.

'*Buona sera, signori e signore*,' she started, and Peroni decided that he liked the voice; it was clear, unaffected, straightforward.

'I should like to sing for you *Nel blu dipinto di blu*.' She bowed slightly, Maurizio made a little twitching motion at the orchestra and they started.

Penso che un sogno così non ritorni mai più—
Mi dipingevo le mani e la faccia di blu . . .

She was no Callas, but there was something very likeable about her way of singing. Like her speaking voice it was unaffected, and if it soared to no lyrical heights there was a pleasing humility about it which let the song come before the singer.

Volare o-o,
Cantare o-o-o . . .

She stood still as she sang, neither conducting an indecorous love affair with the microphone nor making inappropriate gestures with her hands.

. . . poi d'improvviso venivo dal vento rapito
E incominciavo a volare nel cielo infinito . . .

Suddenly Peroni's enjoyment was cut off short. Maurizio, as

he minced about the rostrum, had become aware of Peroni's presence and was now bombarding him with a mute but flaunting courtship. He waggled his hips, darted coy glances at Peroni's table, winked, smoothed back his hair with one hand from the temples to the nape of the neck.

It was only a matter of seconds before somebody would realise this performance was all for Peroni's benefit and then heads would start to turn. The moment had come to spear Captain Gigi. Peroni abandoned his table as if the area had suddenly grown red hot and threaded his way across the densely crowded floor to where the Captain was leaning over a table, ogling his own image in the eyes of its occupants.

'Captain Gigi?'

'*Si*?' The slow roll of the monosyllable indicated that he didn't like customers taking the initiative with him.

'*Questura*,' said Peroni, deliberately sounding and looking like a policeman. He made sure that the word could be heard by everyone within a radius of five metres, at the same time showing his police card with a gesture that any follower of detective films couldn't have failed to recognise.

'I'm busy,' said Captain Gigi, trying to bluster.

'If that's how you want it,' said Peroni, 'I'll take you into the *Questura* and hold you all night for questioning. By morning we should have enough to keep you in till Christmas.'

Captain Gigi realised he was beaten. 'Come with me,' he said.

They moved through the tables towards the back followed by every eye in the place.

Captain Gigi led Peroni through the restaurant to his own office. The fact that the predominant item of furniture in it was a sofa gave Peroni a shrewd idea of the Captain's activities there.

'What can I offer you to drink?' From Captain Gigi's tone of voice and sickening smile it was obvious he had opted for treacle tactics.

'Nothing.'

'Please sit down at least.'

'I prefer to stand. Your name?'

The Captain spread out his pudgy paws and raised his

43

shoulders in an attempt at bonhommie. 'Everybody calls me Captain Gigi.'

'Your real name.'

'Luigi Coliselli.'

Tu sei per me il più bello del mondo—
Un amore profondo
Mi lega a te . . .

Peroni heard Ornella's voice faintly and it did something to attenuate the anger that was gnawing at him.

'What do you know about the disappearance of Kehzia Michaelis?'

'Nothing. What should I know?' There was an air of aggrieved protest in the Captain's tone.

'You couldn't keep your fat paws off her!' This was, Peroni recognised, a non sequitur, but he didn't think the Captain would notice.

At this point something unpleasant happened. An appalling leer spread over Captain Gigi's face and he winked at Peroni a slow and knowing wink. 'You know how it is,' he said.

'No, I don't,' said Peroni, who nevertheless did.

'Girls like that, wandering about the world—they'll do it with anybody.'

A vomit-like heave of jealousy and hatred swelled inside Peroni, and he moved in swiftly to play a Neapolitan gutter trick that would hurt Captain Gigi very much indeed.

Tu sei per me uno caro bambino . . .

Whether it was the sound of Ornella's voice or a decisive intervention of the Commissario he was unable to tell, but he stopped just in time.

'Did she do it with you?' he contented himself with asking.

'No, no . . .'

If he had said yes probably neither the Commissario nor Ornella could have done anything about it; as it was Peroni was left uneasily wondering whether the Captain was lying out of fear. Was there never to be any surety about Kehzia?

'I don't think you tell the truth easily, Coliselli,' he said, 'I think you're one of those people who lie without thinking about

44

it. So I warn you now to start thinking hard. I want true answers to every question I ask, and if I don't get them remember that an unstraight Neapolitan policeman like me with good Mafia contacts has almost unlimited powers for smashing a fancy-dress sailor like you.'

The Neapolitan gutter kid within Peroni sneered at the cheap melodrama of it, but it seemed to work, which was all that mattered.

'When did Kehzia Michaelis first come here?'

'The beginning of June. She asked me for a job as a singer. I said we already had a singer.' He wobbled his folding expanses of chin and neck in the direction from which Ornella's voice was coming. 'Ornella there. Kehzia said that didn't matter—she had her own act with a guitar. She could sing while the band was taking a pause. I listened to her and I realised she was good, so I took her on for the season.'

'How much did you pay her?' asked Peroni and watched the lie jump up and then slide down again discouraged in the Captain's piggy eyes.

'Five thousand lire a night.' It was a slave wage and he knew it. 'She could pick up as much as she wanted from the customers,' he started in a bid to justify himself and then, realising that that line of argument led in a dangerous direction, let it peter out.

But did she pick up as much as she wanted from the customers? Peroni wondered with anguish. Captain Gigi was understandably vague on the point. In fact, he only mentioned one man in connection with Kehzia and that was obviously de Sanctis.

'Did you notice anything at all unusual about her manner in the days immediately before she disappeared?'

Captain Gigi appeared to concentrate. 'As a matter of fact she has been somehow different lately,' he said after a second.

'How different?'

'Strained—as though she was worried about something and half her mind was way off somewhere else. I put it down to—' He stopped, looking frightened.

'You put it down to what?' Another flicking fist of a

45

question.

Captain Gigi licked his whale-blubbery lips and his little eyes, deep sunk in their fleshy wrappings, darted about like lizards in search of escape. 'To drugs,' he said at last.

Peroni felt dread as this new vista opened before him. He foresaw endless skirmishes in the murky half world of drug addiction; young men and women with dead eyes and deader brains staring at the dream of a needle. And at the end of it all would he run down a Kehzia reduced to their level, seeing love as a means to heroin?

'Did she have any friends as far as you know? I don't mean lovers—I mean friends, men or women?'

'Ornella,' said Captain Gigi, 'I've often seen them talking together, eating together. Maybe Ornella was her friend,' Suddenly he saw a chance of getting off the hook. 'Shall I send her to you?'

'Don't worry,' said Peroni, deciding he had had enough of Captain Gigi and that Ornella would make a pleasant change, 'I'll go and find her.'

They left the office in silence and returned to the festivities under the awning. Ornella was no longer singing and, in her place, Maurizio was mincing about the rostrum hugging his concertina. His chubby face lit up when he saw Peroni.

Peroni pretended not to have seen him and looked about for Ornella. She was sitting at a table by herself in a corner drinking a beer, smoking a cigarette and scratching her right foot.

As Peroni started to walk towards her he felt Captain Gigi's look of pure venom searing almost tangibly into the back of his neck.

Seven

It was the strawberries which made her foot itch so badly. Ornella knew she ought to be careful with strawberries, but if you couldn't let yourself go occasionally with something what was the point of living?

The itch was infuriating, too; it was playing hide-and-seek with her fingernails and she knew very well that when she'd scratched the skin all raw it would still be there as frisky as ever.

Suddenly she was aware that somebody was standing over her table. She stopped scratching. A man. She could see the shoes. Maybe German, probably drunk and certainly about to make an immoral suggestion. Such was Ornella's invariable luck.

She let her eyes move slowly up the man's body, at the same time formulating a turn down which would be short and to the point and just about polite.

But some while before she got to the face she realised that for once she was wrong. He was neither German nor drunk and, for the moment at any rate, didn't appear to be on the brink of an immoral suggestion. Then she got to the face and saw that he was also good-looking. Southern, with black eyes which signalled the sort of danger signal that no girl in her right mind would ever try to avoid.

Of course, the chances of anything coming of this meeting were about as good of those of an elderly spinster sneaking off with the leaning tower of Pisa. Ornella's luck on these occasions was about as buoyant as a lead coffin. Look what a flying start she'd got off to—scratching her foot! Still, there was no harm in looking.

All these thoughts went through her head in less than the time it took her to wiggle her foot as unobtrusively as possible back into its shoe.

'*Buona sera*,' she said, dismally failing to sound cool and detached.

'*Buona sera*,' he said with the sort of smile you could live with for a good chunk of eternity. 'Forgive me disturbing you,' he went on, 'I'm from the *Questura*.'

Questura? *Mamma mia*! What could the *Questura* want with her? Then the rising panic was checked when she perceived the probable motive of the visit. 'Is it about Kehzia?'

'That's right.'

'Sit down then, won't you? Let me get you a drink.'

'No, no—let *me* get *you* a drink.'

'Well thanks, if you insist. But make it look as though I'm paying—we get a discount.'

She skilfully hooked a waiter and, while he was ordering, observed him with a mixture of pleasure and curiosity. For some odd reason there seemed to be something familiar about him.

'Forgive me if I sound stupid,' she said, 'but haven't I seen you somewhere before?'

Diffidence? Embarrassment? She couldn't quite interpret his expression.

'I know that if I'd seen *you* before I wouldn't have forgotten,' he countered.

'Wait a minute—it's coming back to me. *Oggi*. I saw your photograph in *Oggi* about a month ago. No, don't tell me—I'll get it by myself.' And suddenly she got it. Her eyes widened and her mouth dropped open. 'Achille Peroni!' she said, 'The Rudolph Valentino of the Italian police! *Mamma mia*! That this should happen to me! Course I should've realised at once—they said you were in Venice. Whatever will *la mamma* say when I tell her?'

Then she pulled herself up short. He must get simply furious with people drooling at him like that. 'Sorry,' she said, 'don't pay any attention to me. Just ask the questions and I'll concentrate on the answers.'

He looked at her for a second and she did her best against

heavy odds to think like a practical and matter-of-fact witness.

'Kehzia is your friend?'

'Yes, she is.'

'What did you think when she didn't turn up the night before last?'

'I was amazed. Oh, Kehzia's a bit crazy in some ways, but when she makes an agreement she sticks to it.'

'Did she ever say anything which suggested she *might* suddenly just leave?'

'No, not exactly . . .'

'But?'

'She did say something about ten days ago which stuck in my mind. I was moaning a bit and saying I was fed up with everything being so *ordinary*. "Ornella," she said, "never complain about the ordinary—it's the bread and water of life. What you want to be careful of is the *extra* ordinary".'

'Did you ask her what she meant?'

'Yes, I did, but she just said "Oh, nothing special" and changed the subject.'

'Have you noticed anything unusual in her manner recently?'

'Well, she's been a bit worried-looking I suppose. Distracted. But we all get a bit like that at times, don't we?' She stopped, confused, realising that she was counting him in with herself and the common run of humanity.

'Yes, we do.' He almost looked as though he were pleased she had counted him in with herself. She felt a sort of wrenching inside—a feeling which always preluded her heart being called into service as a punching bag.

For a second she found herself looking into those dangerous eyes, and then somehow they were back with the questions and answers.

'This distraction of hers,' said Achille Peroni, 'could it have had something to do with drugs?'

Drugs? That had never occurred to her. The whole drug scene was a nightmare world unvisited by her. Every so often you saw thrown away needles on the beach and once she'd seen

49

a boy—quite a good-looking boy—squatting between two bathing huts injecting himself. But Kehzia on drugs?

'I don't know,' she said, 'I suppose it could have had.'

'How did Kehzia feel about Captain Gigi?'

'That pig?' It was a relief to vent her disgust. 'She despised him—same as I do. When he's not eating or drinking or counting his money he's always trying to paw us.'

'But she never let herself—be pawed?'

'Kehzia? Even the idea of it made her sick!' As she said it, Ornella had the odd feeling that he was somehow relieved to hear such an emphatic denial.

'What about other men?'

'She didn't tell me a lot. Sometimes girls don't, you know, between themselves—in spite of what people say. There was a man from Venice—rich I should think.'

'Why do you say "was"—as though he were past?'

'I thought he *was* past.'

'Did she tell you that?'

'Not in so many words—I just had the impression. I think she dropped him when Luca came on the scene.'

'Luca?'

'She's been going about with him quite a bit recently. Much more suitable. And good-looking, too.'

'You've seen him then?'

'Yes. The two of them together. With a priest.'

For an instant Ornella thought she had said something horribly wrong. Achille Peroni suddenly convulsed as though a high voltage current had been put through him. 'Is something the matter?' she asked, scared.

'No,' he said, 'I was just surprised. Can you tell me anything more about the priest?'

'He's the parish priest at the church in Piazza Trento—the *Sacro Cuore di Gesù*.'

'You're sure about that?'

'Quite sure—*la mamma* and I go to Mass there.'

'When was this that you saw them together?'

'About ten days ago.'

'What were they doing?'

'Just talking. I was out shopping and I happened to see Kehzia outside the presbytery with Don Zaccaria and a young man. I admit I was curious, so I went over and said hello. I don't know whether they'd finished talking or whether I broke it up, but Don Zaccaria went back into the presbytery and the three of us went off for an ice-cream. We chatted together for about twenty minutes and I found out that he was called Luca, but otherwise nothing special. And then I went off to get some fish for lunch.'

'Did you ever see him with her again?'

'Yes, a couple of times on the beach.'

'She didn't tell you any more about him?'

'No, and I didn't like to ask. I had a sort of idea they were falling in love.'

For some reason he winced slightly.

'Something the matter?' Ornella enquired sympathetically.

'No, no—just a twinge. One more thing. I'd like you to tell me everything you can about Kehzia as a person. Anything that occurs to you.'

He offered her a pack of English cigarettes which, for some reason, didn't have the stamp on it which all imported packs should have. She took one; he lighted it for her and she inhaled deeply, thinking. It was hard to describe Kehzia.

'She was a restless sort of person,' she said. 'She gave you the impression that she was always looking for something. Or somebody. And that she could never really be happy, or even at peace for a little while, until she'd found that thing or person. Yes, that was it—she was rootless. A gypsy without a tribe. You could hear it in all her songs—the other side of the moon, Atlantis, the seeking of pollen and the migrating of swallows. But in spite of that she had a lovely sense of humour. She could imitate people wonderfully—Captain Gigi and Maurizio, for instance, so that I used to really hurt myself laughing—'

Ornella broke off suddenly, struck by an appalling thought. 'Hey!' she said, 'I've been talking about her in the past, as though she was—' She stopped herself again, not wanting even to say the word. 'But she's not, is she?' she went on like a child asking to be reassured.

51

'I've found no evidence to indicate that she is.'

Or that she isn't. The thought lay heavily between them.

Ornella opened her bag hastily. It was in its usual state of overcrowded chaos and, as she dipped about in it for a handkerchief, she resolved absently and for the umpteenth time to sort through it. Having found the handkerchief she dabbed at her eyes with it.

'Go on,' said Peroni.

'Well, you might say the way I'm feeling now says something about her. She's got a capacity for—arousing other people's fondness.' She stressed the present tense. 'And that's because she can be so fond herself. She's got an endless reserve of affection. She gives it to me. She'll give it to an old beggar in the street, or a child that's cut its knee, or a girl who's trying to sell detergents.'

Ornella paused. There was one more thing to say, but she was curiously reluctant to say it.

'Well?' said Peroni, and she had the uncanny impression that he could read her mind.

'Well,' she said, 'I've got a feeling that there's another side to her. It sounds corny, but I can only describe it as a darker side. She's never really showed it to me, but I can feel it and I'm scared of it. I think she's scared of it, too.'

She came to an end and looked at Achille Peroni. He was absorbed, but somehow it wasn't the absorption of a policeman following the trail of a missing person. There was something different about it which at first she couldn't place. And then in an icy flash it came to her.

It was the absorption of a lover. But it wasn't her he was in love with. It was Kehzia.

I just might have known, thought Ornella, that that unfailing old bad luck of mine would be hanging round to play me one of its usual dirty tricks. I meet the man of a lifetime and he has to be in love with a girl who isn't there.

Madonna santissima, she prayed, don't let him see that I know!

Fortunately it was time for her to sing again. She murmured an apology to Peroni and stood up.

Then as she climbed onto the rostrum she caught herself thinking that maybe it wasn't so hopeless after all. That maybe Kehzia was dead. The thought gave her a twist of pain and she dismissed it as monstrous.

But it had been there.

The Bora

Eight

A buffeting wind was blowing in from the sea, catching up little whirlwinds of sand, tugging at the red flags which the lifeguards had already hoisted to indicate no swimming. The population of the beach was reduced by three-quarters; the remaining quarter adapted themselves to the weather in various ways. Some went jogging along the foreshore; some lay or huddled in small encampments partly protected by deck chairs to catch what little sun was going; some, ignoring the red flags, bobbed and plunged in the foaming, choppy sea.

One elderly man with a handkerchief tied round his head, bare feet and rolled up trousers was involved in a frantic wrestling match with a copy of the Venetian daily paper, the *Gazzettino*. He was trying to turn the page, but the newspaper, aided and abetted by the wind, was doing everything in its power to prevent him. He grabbed it at the top and it billowed out and away from him at the bottom; he clutched at the bottom, and the top streamed, flapping triumphantly, out of his control. He then attempted a wide, all-in wrestling hold around the middle, but his reflexes weren't what they had been twenty years before and one page broke free from his grasp altogether. Holding the remainder in wild disarray he stood up to catch the fugitive, but it soared out of his reach and then plunged inland towards the Hawaii Hotel, so he gave it up as a bad job and sat down again.

Like a demented bird, the sheet of newspaper seemed to be dive-bombing the Hawaii swimming pool, but at the last moment it changed its mind and blew off to the right of it along the street linking the beach with Via Verdi.

Once in Via Verdi it wrapped itself round a tree, but the wind which was obviously following its progress with sympathy came and tugged it free. It scudded over the road, narrowly avoided plastering itself over the windscreen of a passing car and then blew in by the side of the *Pensione* Elena, through the garage space at the rear and over a hedge into the flat, green fields.

Here the force of the wind was somewhat reduced by the buildings between fields and sea, but it obviously had no intention of abandoning its friend, the sheet of newspaper. With a gust here and a billow there it carried it further and further inland on its wild joy-ride to freedom.

Finally it came to a ramshackle, single-storey building with a wooden stall outside and, either because it had tired of the game or because the wind had lost interest, it fluttered to a halt outside the front door where it lay with a local page of Jesolo news upwards.

Half way down this page was a photograph of Kehzia and a story headlined *Police Hunt Missing Girl*.

'It's the Bora,' said Peroni's sister, Assunta. 'It lasts for three days. Pass your sister the biscuits, Stefano.'

'Does that mean we can't swim for three days?'

'It looks like it.'

'Perhaps we could go to Venice for a day-trip,' suggested Anna Maria.

'Or the islands.'

'Or better still do some homework,' suggested Assunta. 'You haven't even started it.'

At this point Peroni, who had spent the night there, came in. Everybody was careful to act as though the previous day's scene had not occurred.

'*Ciao*, Uncle Achille!'

'*Ciao*, Achille. Coffee?'

'Please. What a frightful wind.'

'It's the Bora—it lasts for three days.'

'What did you find out last night?' asked Anna Maria. 'We tried to wait up for you, but you never came!'

'What *did* I find out?' said Peroni trying to make himself sound completely objective. 'That maybe she was on drugs.

That she had a boy-friend called Luca. And that the two of them were seen with a priest who she had also visited on her own.'

'But is she dead of alive? That's the vital thing!'

'I don't know. I just don't know. Maybe I'll find out today.'

Before she had even opened her eyes, Rita heard the sound of the Bora moaning and howling outside. She didn't think of it so much as a wind, but rather as a huge invisible dog which rampaged for three days; and when it came strange things always happened; they might be good and they might be bad, but they were always strange.

Getting up didn't take her long. She pulled on her only skirt and blouse which were at the foot of the bed and shuffled into her only pair of shoes.

As she sucked noisily at the remains of some coffee she had made the night before she wondered vaguely whether she would sell anything today. Her only means of income was the sale of fruit and vegetables she grew herself and vinegary wine which she bought at near giveaway prices and bottled in old flasks. These wares she displayed on the stall outside her house which stood on one of the near deserted little roads criss-crossing the fields behind Jesolo. Throughout the season she spent most of her waking time at this stall waiting for unwary holiday-makers and dreaming or remembering—there was no very clear distinction between the two—the most extraordinary things.

So having finished her coffee she got up creakily to go out to the stall.

But outside the front door the first of the strange things brought by the Bora on its three-day visit was awaiting her. A newspaper. Or rather a sheet of newspaper.

The only bits of newspaper that Rita normally ever saw were those that came wrapped round things. To have one so to speak delivered to the front door was a startling novelty, so she picked it up and studied it carefully.

She had a calendar with pictures of cars for each month, salvaged from a hotel dustbin and this hung in a place of honour in her stall beneath a picture of her namesake, St Rita of

Cascia, the patron saint of the impossible. So now after a studious confrontation of the two she was able to conclude that the paper was today's. Such topicality was almost overwhelming.

She turned her attention to the news contained in it, and was at once struck by the photograph of a dark-haired girl. Now that was an interesting face; that was the face of somebody to whom strange things happened; that was the sort of face that the three-day Bora might well blow in your direction.

What had the owner of that face done? 'P – o – l – i – c – e h – u – n – t m – i – s – s – i – n – g g – i – r – l,' she spelt out slowly. So she was missing; that was hardly to be wondered at with a face like that. Laboriously she started to decipher the story.

'*A twenty-five-year-old American girl, Kehzia Michaelis, has vanished without trace from the tent in which she was living on the beach. Signorina Michaelis was last seen about midnight on Sunday at the Dolce Vita in Jesolo village where her singing to her own guitar accompaniment had become a popular feature. Police have established that she normally caught a bus from Jesolo village to Piazza Nember, then walked along the beach for the last stretch of her journey to her tent, but so far nobody has come forward with information regarding her movements on Sunday night after leaving the Dolce Vita. The investigation is being conducted under the brilliant direction of Commissario Achille . . .*'

Rita's attention was no longer focussed on the newsprint, but was reaching through it towards another scene which was not yet clear.

Sunday night. She hadn't been seen since midnight on Sunday night. And what was it Rita had seen out of the window in the early hours of Monday morning?

With the hot breath of the Bora still panting and snuffling over her she closed her eyes and concentrated. And sure enough it began to come together—the whole scene in silence and slow motion. Extraordinary really she should have forgotten it. But then there were vegetables and coffee and St Rita and mice and mosquitoes and the dust. One couldn't remember everything.

60

Now that the paper had been delivered, however, in the mouth of the Bora things were different. She would have to do something about it.

But what?

The previous day Peroni had asked for a report on Fabrizio and (just to make sure) Marco de Sanctis. This was now waiting for him at the Jesolo police headquarters, but it was not much help. It filled in Fabrizio's playboy background and gave some details of the large personal fortune which even his style of living had been unable seriously to encroach upon, but it revealed no facts or tendencies which might implicate him with the disappearance of Kehzia. The same went for Marco. Peroni sifted in vain through the details of his short career which was now leading up towards an imminent and apparently brilliant degree in geology at Ferrara University. De Sanctis, father and son, were wealthy, outstanding and apparently quite unimpeachable. There was only Peroni's overwhelmingly strong impression that Fabrizio was in love with Kehzia. If that were so could it have induced him to murder her? The possibility stood like a nightmare statue at the crossroads of Peroni's mind, demanding his attention. Then, while he was reluctantly studying it, he was informed that somebody wished to see him about Kehzia Michaelis.

The person turned out to be altogether unexpected. She must have been about eighty with wrinkled skin, hardened and browned by weather, skimpy white hair and dark brown eyes that were surprisingly bright, almost like those of some small forest animal. Her clothes seemed to have seen almost as much service as she had done herself. Each finger-nail was lined with a sort of picture frame of black and a distinctly characteristic odour wafted from her. In one hand she clutched a sheet of newspaper.

'Monday morning,' she said, 'something woke me early. I'm a very light sleeper, your honour, always have been. Even as a girl in Jesolo village. That's where I was born—Jesolo village. And lived there till my husband died twenty years ago,' she crossed herself reverently, 'and I set up my stall here at the lido . . . '

How to stop her? thought Peroni, who had fallen quite unconsciously into the role of a benevolent social worker. The old woman had been brought into him some minutes before on the grounds that she had something to say concerning Kehzia Michaelis, but the nearest they had got so far was that she had been woken up on Monday morning early.

' . . . and it's a funny thing, your honour, I can remember everything that happened all those years ago in Jesolo village, but you ask me what happened yesterday and like as not I've clean forgotten it!'

'And Monday morning?' Peroni prompted gently.

'Monday morning? Ah yes, Monday morning. As I was saying, your honour, something woke me up early. So I got out of bed and went to see what the weather was like. Because the weather's important, your honour. I've always believed in the weather. Some people go by the stars, but don't you take any notice of them. It's the weather you want to watch.'

'You went to the window,' said Peroni with the limitless patience of a social worker with a vocation.

'I went to the window? Yes, that's right, your honour, I went to the window. And I looked out of the window.' Suddenly she seemed to lose all desire to wander and she held Peroni with the glittering eye of the Ancient Mariner. 'And that was when I saw it!'

'Saw what?'

'The building as lies across the field from my house!'

Having said this in a dramatic whisper she came to a full stop. Peroni decided she must be mad. 'Thank you very much for coming to tell me, Signora,' he said, half rising from his chair.

But, as though she had taken off a gramophone record and put on the other side of it, the story was now resumed. 'And outside the building as lies across the field from my house there was some cars.'

'Is there any reason why there shouldn't be some cars outside the building?' Peroni enquired politely.

'There is, your honour,' she said, 'because there's nobody lives there.'

He had to admit she had scored a point this time.

'And I knows what goes on in that building, see?' she went on.

'What does go on there?'

'They stick needles into themselves.'

Maybe she wasn't mad after all.

'Who stick needles into themselves?'

'The Russians—the ones who were exploding bombs here a couple of months ago.'

The needle swung back towards insanity.

'And what did you see out of your window, apart from the building and the cars?'

Again she fixed him with a beady eye. 'At first nothing,' she said. 'And then nothing again. And then the door a-opens and a man comes out and looks all about him. And then the man beckons to somebody inside. And another man comes out carrying a girl in his arms.'

She paused, her eye still locked with Peroni's and then suddenly slammed down on the desk the sheet of newspaper she was carrying. 'That girl,' she said, stubbing her finger at Kehzia's picture.

'How can you be so sure it was that girl?'

'Same hair, same face.'

'And then what happened?'

'The second man put her in the back of one of the cars and got in the front and drove off. That was all.'

There was a chilly verisimilitude about the story. Peroni had seen it all as she recounted it, like a film without sound track. The empty building, silent in the flat, dawn landscape with the cars that shouldn't have been there parked outside. And then nothing, and then nothing again, and finally the door opening for the appearance of the beckoning figure and that other figure with the girl in his arms.

'Could you see why he was carrying her?' asked Peroni. 'Was she asleep or what?'

'Oh no,' said the old woman, 'she was dead.'

63

Nine

The police car halted on the deserted side-road outside the hut with the fruit and vegetable stall in front of it, and Peroni and the young detective, Roberti, got out with some relief, as close proximity to Rita had become a strain on the olfactory sense.

The fields stretched out all about them, their long grass ruffled and tossed by the Bora. Not a soul was in sight except for themselves and the only sound was the howling of the wind. About a kilometre away, blocking off the sea, was Jesolo lido like the rear view of a stage setting.

Already the bone-deep gash which the old woman named Rita had inflicted on Peroni's hopes was beginning to heal itself. Maybe the whole thing was an invention, he told himself. And even if there were some truth in it, how could she possibly be sure that the girl was Kehzia with nothing more than a newspaper photograph to go on? And finally, even assuming the identification were correct, it was absurd to believe that Rita could accurately diagnose death at a distance and by the dawn light.

'It's all a bit of a mess, your honours,' Rita was saying, 'I don't get much time to tidy up. I'm too busy running the stall, you see . . .'

'Is that the building you meant?' Peroni interrupted gently, pointing at another one-storey construction, not unlike Rita's home, standing about fifty metres off.

'That's the one, your honour.'

'We'll just go and have a look at it,' said Peroni.

'Could she possibly have recognised the Michaelis girl at this distance?' asked Roberti when they were out of earshot. 'By dawn light, too.'

'That's what I was thinking,' said Peroni. But if her eyesight was good, a chill voice whispered inside him, and the sun had been over the horizon, then recognition wouldn't have been impossible.

'*Dottore*—'

Peroni—not a doctor of medicine, but of law like practically everybody else at the *Questura*—looked where Roberti was pointing. There were clear signs of tyre tracks in the grass. It wasn't conclusive, of course; cars were parked everywhere; the last word lay with the building itself, and this Peroni hoped to find impregnably barred, shuttered and locked.

He was disappointed. There was a snapped-off padlock hanging on the front door and when they took that off the door opened without any trouble. Then, as soon as they'd stepped inside, Peroni saw with a lurch of dread that a good part at least of Rita's story was true.

The floor was covered with syringes. And littered among them were empty Coke cans and crumpled up packs of American cigarettes.

With a desolate sense of foreboding Peroni saw another piece of the picture falling into place. Rita's Russians had been Americans, an understandable enough substitution given the Alice in Wonderland state of her mind. And the bombs? Probably just colourful embroidery.

They went over the whole building centimetre by centimetre, but without finding out any more than they had learned in the first instant: the place had been used by Americans for at least one collective trip on hard drugs, probably heroin. Finally they collected the syringes for analysis and went outside.

'Get in touch with the American Military Police, *dottore*,' said Peroni as they were driving back to Jesolo police head-quarters. 'We want to know all we can about the drug scene on the American base in Vicenza because that's almost certainly where they come from. Trace all the American servicemen who were in Jesolo during Sunday night. The chief priority now is to find as many people as possible who were at that party.'

The photographer, Benito Mussolini, got through an in-ordinate amount of coffee. Twenty-five cups of the stuff a day, powerful and concentrated, was nothing to him. He started on it as soon as he woke in the morning and thereafter the rest of the day was punctuated with it like a rambling sentence with commas. He nipped out of the shop for it to the bar next door and when he was out taking photographs he always knew with his eyes closed exactly where the nearest bar was. Desdemona, his monkey, was addicted, too, and would sit on his shoulder or the bar counter making little pleading noises until he poured out some for her in the saucer.

This morning, however, Desdemona was fast asleep in her high chair behind the counter, so Benito tiptoed out of the shop, hung up the *Vengo Subito* notice and went next door.

When he had his coffee he picked up the bar copy of the *Gazzettino* and started to leaf through it. He never bought a newspaper, but made a point of going through somebody else's every day.

General Calamari denies bribe allegations. Etna in full eruption. New government crisis tomorrow? General strike next week. Twenty terrorists escape from jail in mass break-out. Nothing as usual.

And then he turned a page and a face jumped out at him. The fact that it was an attractive female face meant nothing to him; he wasn't interested in attractive female faces. But somewhere before he had seen it and Benito Mussolini never forgot a face once seen. He filed them all away for possible future use and such was the efficiency of his mental computer that sooner or later he was invariably able to fit them into a background.

He turned to the story concerning the face. *Twenty-five-year-old American girl . . . vanished without trace . . . tent on the beach . . . Dolce Vita . . .* His eyes filleted the story in search of some detail that, fed into the computer, would bring up the background against which he had seen the face. But without results.

The fact that he couldn't remember her at once almost certainly meant that she had played no speaking role in his existence. And, in its turn, *that* meant that she was one of the large army of people he had only seen through the lens of his camera. They were much more difficult to recall, but sooner or

66

later he always traced them.

He got another coffee, lit a new cigarette from the stub of the old and closed his eyes in concentration.

On his return from old Rita's Peroni found awaiting him two surprises which partly distracted his mind from the desolate prospect of Kehzia having died from a drug overdose. First, he learned on making enquiries that old Rita's bombs were not quite such embroidery after all. There had been several reports of explosions in the semi-wasteland behind the lido a couple of months previously, but the explosions had stopped as unaccountably as they had started and the police had assumed that those responsible were holiday-makers who had subsequently left Jesolo.

Then, no sooner had he taken in this news than Peroni was told there was a call for him from de Sanctis in Venice. Curious, with at the same time that taut feeling which told him something new and perhaps important was about to happen, he picked up the receiver.

'*Pronto*?'

'Commissario Peroni?'

'Speaking.'

'It occurred to me after you'd left yesterday, Commissario, that I'm holding a small dinner party this evening which would be greatly enhanced if you would attend it.'

'I'm afraid I shall be on duty this evening.'

'There will be some interesting guests there. I'm sure you would find it a most rewarding experience.'

That dangerous final adjective. There was no need of anything more specific for Peroni to understand he was being offered a bribe, and a big one at that. But why? And why now? What had happened in the past twenty-four hours to make de Sanctis think Peroni worth bribing? The answer to that could well be of vital assistance in dissipating the mystery that surrounded Kehzia. Was that the reason he felt so strongly tempted to accept? Or was it rather the lure of the bribe itself? The old Peroni jostled the new one with insolent insistence.

'I shall be on duty,' he limited himself to repeating.

67

At this point de Sanctis mentioned a name. It was a very big name indeed and its owner, Peroni was assured, would not only be present at the dinner, but was most anxious to make Peroni's acquaintance.

'Half-past eight,' said de Sanctis.

At that there came the click of the receiver being put down. The invitation was wide open. But Peroni, as he firmly reminded himself, would of course ignore it.

He set himself to thinking of Kehzia and found that he was willing it not to be her that old Rita had seen in the man's arms. The investigation into the American drug party would have to go forward, of course. In the meantime he intended continuing the mainstream enquiries. And here there was one, possibly vital, aspect which had been left totally uncovered. This concerned the mysterious young man called Luca who, Ornella believed, Kehzia had been falling in love with. So now, in an attempt to learn more of Luca, Peroni set off once again for the presbytery.

As before the door was opened by Teodorico Bo. The sacristan's expression remained unchanged when he saw Peroni; the black eyes just stared, but hostility seeped out of him like a cloud.

'Don Zaccaria?' said Peroni, at the same time reading Bo's mental reaction. "I cannot shut the door in the face of this southern busybody. I must receive him. But I will not show him the smallest hint of politeness. I will watch him as unfailingly as circumstances allow and will eavesdrop on him if I can. Above all I will do everything in my power to see that he learns nothing of the things I know."

But what were the things that Bo knew?

Without word or gesture, the sacristan allowed Peroni to enter the hall and then held open the door of the study for him, closing it again when he was inside.

As he waited, Peroni looked at the military-looking saints whose pictures hung on the walls and he wondered ridiculously whether they could give him some clue as to the secrets of Don Zaccaria and his sacristan; but they remained strictly to attention with their lips sealed as though they were under orders

68

to keep silence at all costs.

And then Don Zaccaria glided into the room. Considering his large, horsey frame, he was remarkably silent in his movements. He looked annoyed to see Peroni, but Peroni had been expecting that.

'I'm sorry to trouble you again.'

Don Zaccaria inclined his long head in acknowledgement of the apology, at the same time gesturing for Peroni to sit.

'What can I do for you?'

'I'm trying to trace a young man named Luca who was friendly with Kehzia Michaelis.'

Peroni noticed with mild irritation that he was unable to avoid that same confessional tone he had fallen into before.

'Why do you suppose that I know anything of him?'

'You were seen together with the pair of them.'

There was no change in the expression of the sagging, melancholy eyes, but Peroni could tell that he had scored a point. Don Zaccaria picked up a magnifying glass and studied it intently as though he were interrogating it upon some fine point of canon law; then he put it down again in its exact previous position. Finally he gave a soft, meditative whinny which appeared to announce that he had reached a decision.

'I do know of the young man you refer to,' he said.

Ah, but you wouldn't have told me if Ornella hadn't seen you with him, thought Peroni, but outwardly he merely inclined his head, a submissive penitent accepting good counsel.

'In fact it was through him that Signorina Kehzia came to me.'

Peroni cocked a mental eyebrow at this; maybe they were getting somewhere at last.

'She was in need of guidance,' Don Zaccaria went on, 'and he brought her to see me.'

'Can you be more explicit?'

'Not without the authority of the Cardinal Patriarch.'

Up against the same ecclesiastical brick wall as before.

'What is Luca's surname?'

'Zambelli.'

'How can I get in touch with him?'

69

Again the communing with the magnifying glass followed by an almost whispered neigh of resolution. 'You'll be able to find him at the summer camp for deaf and dumb children run by the Sacred Heart nuns. He helps out there.'

Peroni got up, restraining an instinct to cross himself as though after absolution.

'There's just one more thing I should tell you,' said Don Zaccaria. 'The young man is training for the priesthood.'

Slowly it was coming to him. He had taken her photograph, and not too long ago either.

Benito Mussolini's photography fell into two categories: the work he did in the streets and the work he did in pizzerias and restaurants. In the streets he plumped Desdemona into the arms of individuals before snapping them, but indoors he liked to take entire tablefuls of people at a time (if one didn't buy, another would). And as he had no recollection of forcing Desdemona into the girl's arms, he thought it probable he had taken her seated at table.

With somebody else.

Here Benito Mussolini's calculations collapsed like a fast spinning top halted by a hand. And always the same hand. The missing negatives were still missing, so how could he ever find out who had been with the girl?

And then something else occurred to him. On the night before his shop had been broken into he had taken a series of photographs in a pizzeria called the Far West of a large, German package deal group. The leader of the group had asked him to develop these overnight as the party was leaving for Germany next morning.

Rather than sort out the package deal negatives from those of other people in the Far West he had decided to develop them all; with seven-eighths of the pizzeria occupied by the Germans the sales percentage would still be vastly higher than normal, even if none of the others bought. Then the next morning the package deal group would collect their photographs according to the numbered slips while the remaining photographs would be—

Where?

Benito Mussolini's mind pounded like a rat on a treadmill to remember where he had put those other photographs.

But his memory, so unerring for faces, was defective in other things. He couldn't remember where they'd ended up.

Quickly he paid for his coffees, lit a third cigarette from the stub of the second one and ran next door, snatching down the *Vengo Subito* sign as he went in.

Desdemona had woken in his absence and climbed onto the counter to wait for him. Now, as she saw him, she started to chatter excitedly and jump up and down waving her arms.

'*Ciao, tesoro*,' he said, kissing her absently. 'What's that? No, I wasn't—I was only next door having a coffee. Well, I didn't like to wake you. All right, next time I will. Now be quiet a minute, *angelo*—I've got to think . . .'

He looked through the drawers behind the counter without much hope; they were kept for developed work scheduled for delivery. Then he tried the shelves where he kept frames and films. Not there, either. Desdemona was in a state of high excitement, jumping about between her chair and the counter making whimpering noises.

'Some photographs,' said Benito, apparently in answer to her, 'some photographs I put away somewhere, *tesoro*.' More whimpering. 'Well, yes, they just might be important. Or one of them might.'

He went into the back room, switched on the light and started sorting through the piles of stuff which had accumulated out there.

'What's that, *stella mia*?' he said. 'I can't hear you. I keep saying it's no good talking to me from one room to another— you know I'm a bit hard of hearing in one ear.'

Desdemona arrived chattering in a state of high excitement and started swinging from the table with one arm.

'That red and gold harness we saw in the window, *angelo*?' said Benito. 'Well, all right—but only if you find them for me, mind.'

Desdemona swung off the table and ran bandily into the front of the shop again.

'Don't turn everything upside down!' he shouted after her.

71

He had started to look through the contents of a promising looking carton when he was interrupted by a series of triumphant squeals from Desdemona.

'You've found them?' he said. 'I don't believe you. I looked everywhere out there.'

Nevertheless he abandoned the carton and followed her into the front of the shop where he found her jumping up and down with excitement clutching some photographs in her hand. These she hurled at him as he approached her.

'But where were they, *tesoro*?' he said.

In answer she banged at her chair, and then he remembered. He had slipped the photographs into the little space between the seat and the back, ironically enough so as to remember where they were. An excellent hiding place.

'*Grazie, angelo*,' he said picking them up.

Leaning on the counter where she had climbed up to participate he started to look through the pictures. At the fourth he stopped. There, at a table in the Far West, was unmistakably the American girl. And she was accompanied by not one, but two people.

'And the pity of it is,' said Benito to Desdemona, 'I haven't the faintest clue as to who either of them could be.'

Ten

The large white building stood way back from the road towards the end of the pine-wood, aloof from the overcrowded jangle of Jesolo. Peroni drove in through the gates and up the long drive. The whole place seemed abandoned. The grounds in front of the house were untended and the building itself was dilapidated, but then it must be difficult to keep up a place that size, even if you were a religious order.

Peroni pulled the heavy bell and heard it clanging dramatically within. Otherwise silence. Silence, indeed, seemed to dominate here unchallenged except for the soughing of the Bora in the pine trees.

For a long time nothing happened, but then the door opened and he saw a nun dressed in white from head to foot and looking very cool. She had gold-rimmed spectacles and a smooth, ageless face.

'*Questura,*' said Peroni delicately. When presenting himself to nuns in his official capacity he was always worried they might be alarmed; they never were. 'I need to speak to a young man by the name of Luca Zambelli.'

That didn't seem to worry her either. She gestured to him to enter, said, 'Follow me,' and glided across the hall and down a corridor as though she had been on silent roller skates. Peroni followed, noticing that the building was much less dilapidated within than without; he thought it might have belonged to some rich family in the last century and then left to the Sacred Heart nuns as the family finally dwindled out with a last remaining pious spinster.

The nun opened a door at the back and they stepped out onto a terrace overlooking the beach and into the full, warm blast of the Bora.

On the blowing and eddying sand and on the foreshore against a background of off-white, angry-looking waves were about fifty children, aged roughly between ten and fifteen. They were engaged in various games, throwing beach balls and Frisbees, playing beach tennis and a variety of bowls, flying kites with the co-operative Bora, digging and building in the sand. At a glance they might have been any group of children at a holiday camp. And then you noticed that their actions were continually interwoven with the swift, bird-like motions of their hands and fingers as they communicated. Unless he had seen it, thought Peroni, he would not have believed that deaf and dumb language could be so vivacious.

There were two adults with this party of children. One of them was another nun dressed all in white with the wind tugging furiously at her habit; the other was a tall, good-looking man who was playing football with a small group of boys. This must be Luca Zambelli, even though he was somewhat older than Peroni had expected: somewhere in his early thirties.

Peroni walked down the steps from the terrace and across the sand, very conscious of the fact that a lot of the darting hands were talking about him.

'Signor Zambelli?'

'*Si* . . . '

He had a pleasant, open face; a thick crop of fair hair, ruffled by the wind; a small colony of freckles about his nose, and grey eyes in which Peroni noticed apprehension.

'*Questura.*'

He didn't even try to feign surprise, and Peroni guessed that Don Zaccaria had spoken to him.

A large ball flew past them, narrowly missing Peroni. Luca caught it and kicked it away, and then by mutual consent the two of them walked down the beach away from the children.

'It's about Kehzia?'

'Yes. When did you hear she'd disappeared?'

'I've only just found out.'

'How?'

'I saw it in the paper.'

Too glib. Besides, as he came through the house Peroni had

spotted a copy of the Catholic daily *Avvenire* which wouldn't have carried the story at all; no sign of the local *Gazzettino*. Not that it mattered.

'When did you last see her?'

'On Saturday night. We had a quick supper together.'

'You've heard nothing of her since?'

'No.'

'That didn't surprise you?'

'Not really. You see, I've been very busy here over the weekend and we were due to meet this evening.'

There was a check in his voice as he spoke the last words and Peroni sensed real consternation.

'When did you first meet her?'

He thought for a second. 'Just over two weeks ago,' he said, as though surprised it should be so short a space of time.

'How?' asked Peroni. How did a young man training for the priesthood meet a footloose American girl singing in a place like the Dolce Vita?

Luca seemed a little bewildered by the question, too. 'Well, it was a sort of series of coincidences,' he said awkwardly. 'One day I took a group of children on a trip to Venice and I found myself sitting next to this dark-haired girl on the bus to Punta Sabbioni. Then we were opposite each other on the boat. Then we happened to cross at the Accademia—she was with a man then, but we couldn't help seeing each other.'

'Can you describe the man?'

Luca gave a description which neatly fitted de Sanctis.

'When we were having something to eat in St Mark's Square,' Luca continued at Peroni's request, 'she came right by us with the same man. And so on. We must have crossed each other's paths about half a dozen times during the day. I suppose it's not all that extraordinary. People do tend to run into each other several times when they go for a day in Venice.'

Peroni thought he could detect a note of self-justification, and he remembered once again that the young man was training to be a priest.

'Anyway,' Luca was continuing, 'when we got back here I forgot all about it. Then the next evening I had to go into Jesolo village to pick up an electric slicer that was being repaired there, and I thought I'd have a pizza. So I went into the first pizzeria I saw and there was the same girl singing. She sang very well.' He paused, hearing her. 'When she'd finished,' he went on after a second, 'she had to pass my table. I stood up. We couldn't very well ignore each other.' Peroni caught the same note of self-justification. 'She said, "Are you following me or am I following you?"'

He said the last sentence with the air of somebody recalling a cherished memory, and Peroni realised he had found another source of painful jealousy: was there to be no end of them?

'Well, I offered her a drink and we started talking,' he continued in a rush, 'We got on very well together—like brother and sister really.'

Against a background of howling wind and pounding sea, the last phrase was pure music to Peroni for about a second until he started doubting its genuineness. After all, what better appearance could a seminarist lend to his friendship with a girl than that of a brother and sister relationship?

'So that was how we met,' Luca finished flatly.

'You've seen her often since?'

'Four or five times.' And then, as though that should seem too often, he added quickly, 'A couple of those times I accompanied her to see a priest.'

'Don Zaccaria,' said Peroni, 'I was coming to that. Why did you take her to see him?'

'For instruction.'

The answer tumbled out pre-packed.

'She wanted to become a Catholic?'

'Maybe . . .'

Peroni knew he was up against the same barrier he had faced with Don Zaccaria and even if Luca didn't trump any further questions with a Cardinal Patriarch he would be no less intractable. That aspect of Kehzia would have to be approached from another direction.

'When you last saw her, on Saturday, how did she seem?'

'Much as usual. Perhaps a bit—strained.'

'What sort of strain?'

'I don't know.'

'Drugs?'

At point-blank range the monosyllable had a shattering effect on him. 'No!' he shouted disbelievingly into the teeth of the wind and then, more doubtfully but with no less anguish, 'No—o . . .'

'*Could* she have been?'

Peroni could see him going back over the course of their relationship, examining incidents, phrases, gestures in the light of this new, appalling interpretation. 'She *could* have been, I suppose . . .'

'You said she sang well,' said Peroni switching suddenly as though to take the whole problem by surprise. 'Can you tell me more about that?'

'I can let you hear her,' said Luca so that it was Peroni who was taken by surprise. 'I recorded a tape of her songs.'

Mrs Lynn Randerheim had never been quite the same since her husband, a U.S. army colonel, had been posted to Europe. She had immediately gone way over the moon for European culture. And stayed there. Art, music, literature, drama, ballet, opera, architecture—her seemingly insatiable appetite for things cultural swallowed them all. And languages, too. Mrs Randerheim had taken to Italian as a duck takes to *acqua*.

Colonel Randerheim, who thought that a symphony was a furniture removal van and considered that anyone who spoke anything other than undiluted American was unpatriotic or crazy, had much to put up with. So he was the more astonished when his wife's linguistic abilities were spotted and appreciated by a body which even he couldn't accuse of being un-American or un-hard-headed. The Military Police, in fact, had asked her to interpret when a U.S. serviceman was arrested by the Italian police for stealing a car. The occasion had gone off triumphantly and now whenever the MPs wanted any interpreting done they asked Mrs Randerheim who complied most readily as it provided her with an endless source of dinner party anecdotes.

If all Mrs Randerheim's interpretations took her out of the ordinary, today's did so rather more than usual. For one thing it involved a drive over to Jesolo. For another it allowed her to meet a Man who deserved a capital M as high as the Empire State Building. But when it came to describing him later, she realised, she was going to have trouble. He was hard to pin down with words.

A sort of Mastroianni? No. Gian Maria Volontè? Not him either. Rosanno Brazzi? No, no—way out! You couldn't really compare him to anybody. He was a sort of quintessence of Latin masculinity, and that sounded good, too.

She didn't have long to consider the problem, however, for the American side of the interview, who looked a bit like a Schnauzer, was brought in and she had to concentrate on her interpreting.

The interview opened with a series of routine questions which the American answered with surly suspicion, shifting gum ostentatiously from side to side in his mouth. But as they went on Mrs Randerheim noticed with surprise that the quintessence of Latin masculinity seemed in some curious, chameleon fashion to have changed character. She had once met a very senior officer whose manner was as mild as a pack of pure-air cigarettes, but who only had to look at a GI for him to start curling up like a bug in a cloud of insecticide. That was who he reminded her of now.

'Please tell him,' said the officer in Italian, 'that I want to talk about a heroin party at a building in the fields behind Jesolo lido on Sunday night.'

She repeated the message in English.

'I ain't even heard of no heroin party,' said the Schnauzer with hostility.

'Please tell him,' said the officer, 'that Italian laws relating to drug offences are very severe. I know he was at that party and I could get him several years for it if I tried. So far no charges have been brought. If he wants things to stay that way he'd better start collaborating as quickly and thoroughly as he can manage.'

Mrs Randerheim adjusted her pink-rimmed spectacles uneasily as she translated, feeling almost as though some of the menace had spilled onto her.

78

'OK,' said the Schnauzer after an instant's reflection, 'I was there.'

'Ask him who else was there.'

'A group of guys from the base.'

'Were there any women present?'

'Most of the way it was all guys, but after maybe two-three hours when most of the fellers were blown a chick came in.'

'Alone?'

'No, she had a guy with her.'

'Describe her.'

'Well, she was pretty lush—long, black hair. Maybe about twenty-five, twenty-six. Not too tall.'

The officer showed him a photograph. 'Is that her?'

The Schnauzer studied it carefully. 'Could be,' he said at length. 'It's kinda difficult to be sure.'

'Italian?'

'No, American.'

For an instant it seemed to Mrs Randerheim as though the officer had received a piece of bad news.

'Did you catch her name?'

'Well, kinda. The guy she was with called her something that sounded like Cheea.'

The officer looked up with a jerk and an expression Mrs Randerheim couldn't interpret. 'Cheea?' he said. 'Is he sure of that?'

'That's what it sounded like.'

'Could it have been Kehzia?'

'Yeah, I guess it could.'

More bad news, and worse than the previous piece. It was as though he were personally involved with this girl. For pete's sake, what was going on?

'Did any of the other people at the party know her?'

'I guess not. Though most of them were stoned out of their minds by the time she got there. They wouldn't have known their own mothers.'

'The man she was with—did you know him?'

'Nope.'

'What was he like?'

'A big guy—like a boxer.'

'So as far as you know he didn't come from the Vicenza base?'

'That's right.'

'But the others did?'

'I didn't know them all. Most of them did.'

'This girl—did she have a heroin injection?'

'Yeah, but I reckon she'd already fixed herself good before she got there. She was high as a kite.'

'What happened after she got there?'

'Well, right after she got there I can't tell you what happened because I went off on a trip on my own. But when I got back—I don't know how much later it was—I saw the big guy talking to another of the guys. The chick was lying on the ground and, although I couldn't see her face, I reckoned she must be pretty bad. The second guy went to the door and looked out. Then he beckoned to the big guy who picked up the chick in his arms and carried her out. Coupla seconds after that I heard one of the cars driving off and the second guy came back in.'

'When the big man went out with the girl in his arms, did you manage to see anything of her?'

'Yeah, I caught a glimpse of her face.'

'What sort of condition did she seem to be in?'

'Well, I reckoned she was dead.'

The impression conveyed via the pink-rimmed spectacles to Mrs Randerheim's brain was that the officer's world had come to an abrupt end.

One night I fell in a deep, deep sleep
And the little flames came out of that sleep
And the little flames became a great fire
And the little flames were my funeral pyre.

Who will light the fire
Who will light the fire
Who will light the fire
To save me from the fire?

80

Peroni sat alone in his sister's apartment listening to Kehzia's now for ever stilled voice coming from Anna Maria's tape recorder. It was the voice he had known she would have. Very feminine, a little husky with a hint of infinite longing.

He had seen Kehzia's image, first in photographs and then, more significantly, through the eyes of Ornella and Luca. Now he was hearing her voice and something too—since she had composed the songs—of the mind and heart behind that voice. One more step towards the reality of Kehzia, and with each step he fell more hopelessly in love with her.

But they were steps along a dead end. Towards an end that was literally dead.

One night I flew in a high, high sky
And the little breezes came out of that sky
And the little breezes became a great wind
And the little breezes were my storm-tossed end.

But the investigation had to be continued. Everything had to be checked. All the other people at that party would have to be found. The American's story would have to be confirmed and amplified. The big man who looked like a boxer would have to be traced. All hopelessly.

Who will blow the wind
Who will blow the wind
Who will blow the wind
To save me from the wind?

The hopelessness of it weighed lead-heavy on Peroni. The quest for Kehzia had been more than a mere hunt for a missing person, even a missing person as fascinating as she was. It had become a sort of Grail quest in which the complete Peroni had been caught up. And now that the hope of the Grail had gone he felt as though he had fallen back into a whole drama full of separate characters.

One night I swam in a dark, dark lake
And the little waves came out of the lake . . .

Fundamentally there were two Peronis growing from a single

81

root, like a tree split in two by lightning. There was the *scugnizzo*, the Neapolitan gutter-kid: amoral, irreverent, irrepressible with a bright and unsleeping eye to the main chance whatever irregularities, or worse, might be necessary to attain it. But then, ever since the lighting bolt of truth had struck, an alien Peroni had been growing alongside the *scugnizzo*: *dott* Peroni, Commissario Peroni, the police functionary who believed in correctness and northern-ness.

And then, like branches growing from the main, split trunk there were half a dozen other Peronis as well. Peroni the unashamed lecher, Peroni the courtly lover, Peroni the doting uncle, Peroni the idol of the media, Peroni the anglophilic *bon viveur* . . . There was no end to them.

And the little waves became a great sea . . .

All these Peronis had been fused into a united, aspiring trunk by the quest for Kehzia. But now the unity was gone and there was nothing left to hold Peroni together. In losing Kehzia he had lost himself.

Then a thought crossed his attention slant-wise reminding him that this evening there was the dinner party given by de Sanctis. Before he had fully purposed not to go, but now that Kehzia was dead there was no longer any reason why that purpose should hold.

And the little waves were the end of me.

The Blackbird

Eleven

With a sword the man known as de Sanctis traced a circle round the floor of the large room.

His senses dulled by the lengthy and exquisite meal and the large quantities of alcohol consumed during it, Peroni watched the operation in bewilderment from the doorway, while the others were already grouped inside. He was, he realised, a little drunk.

De Sanctis traced with a charcoal two further concentric circles within the large one and then within the space between these two inner circles he wrote the letters C A Y M.

A party game? It seemed improbable, but what else could it be? Peroni wished he had drunk less.

Next de Sanctis drew four star shapes outside the outer circle in positions more or less corresponding to the four points of the compass. That done he placed a bronze container within the circle and put a match to something in it. Almost immediately smoke began to curl upwards, at first wispily, then more and more densely, and with it came a heavy, exotic, almost sickly odour.

As the sense of luxurious well-being which had suffused him only a few minutes before gave way more and more rapidly to acute misgiving, Peroni began to understand what was going on.

Finally de Sanctis took some objects from a cupboard built into the massive bookcase and placed them on the four star shapes which he had traced at the cardinal points. Peering in the half light, Peroni recognised them with a mixture of disgust and dread as the corpse of a bat, a human skull, the head of a cat and a pair of horns which looked like those of a goat.

'Please step inside the circle, Commissario,' said de Sanctis,

'To stay outside can be dangerous.'

With a dull sense of impotence Peroni realised that he was morally shackled from head to foot. It had all been deliberately planned and there was now no escape from participation in something he found both absurd and repulsive.

He stepped inside the circle.

The evening had started in an altogether different key, a dominant major conveying buoyancy and hope. On arrival at the magnificent island palace near *Campo SS Giovanni e Paolo* he had been taken up by lift to the third floor and then out onto a large roof-terrace dominating the whole of Venice. You could see the five domes of St Mark's, like swelling breasts and the campanile rigid beside them; you could see the doge's palace and the Salute; you could see hundreds of other humbler Venetian roofs and towers, tumbling and clambering over each other in a riotous game of architectural leapfrog.

Was it mere coincidence, in view of what was to happen later, that a phrase about all the kingdoms of the world and the glory of them should have made an uninvited appearance in Peroni's mind?

The Bora, still blowing with malicious insistence in Jesolo, made itself less felt here in Venice, and the party was further protected by a latticework screen densely interwoven with wistaria. The sky was overcast and the temperature heavily oppressive, but the champagne which was so freely circulating as an aperitif was ice-cold.

'Good evening, Commissario,' he had heard himself addressed on arrival, recognising the slightly drawling voice of Marco which always sounded as though it were secretly amused at something. 'Help yourself to champagne and then come and see our aerial view of Venice.'

The view of the Serenissima Republic stretching beneath them was indeed superb, but it didn't prevent Peroni from observing his fellow guests as well. His attention was particularly drawn by a man of powerful bulk with bushy eyebrows and jelly-quivering jowls—the owner of the name de Sanctis had mentioned on the telephone. He was a minister and one of the most powerful figures on the Italian political scene, widely tipped as the next head of government.

As Peroni was looking at him, there erupted on to the terrace a flabby, horse-toothed figure wearing a crimson suit with glittering gold lapels. 'That's Dino Dini, isn't it?' said Peroni.

'That's right. Papa's acquaintances are of all extractions.'

Dino Dini was a stage and television comedian, famous for his racy jokes, outrageous clothes and the loud bray which he used for a laugh. He was engaged in unleashing this bray on his arrival, and the whole of Venice seemed to ring with it.

'Haven't I seen that man somewhere before?' said Peroni, indicating with his eyes a lean, masculine figure with a sharp sardonic face, wearing a smoking jacket and black tie and smoking a cigar.

'Bamboozled, Commissario,' said Marco, 'but by no means the first. It isn't a man at all—it's a woman. The Principessa Guinzinelli.'

'The Principessa Guinzinelli?' echoed Peroni, who had heard the name but couldn't place it.

'What the newspapers describe as a jet-set figure,' explained Marco, 'but industrious with it. She owns the Meta chain-stores. Runs 'em personally. Rumour has it she prices every single object herself. And the lady she's just started talking with is the Contessa Nicolini.'

The Contessa was in no way less startling than the Principessa, though in more classical style. She must have been in her fifties, but still had a potent charge of feminine fascination. Peroni could almost smell it. She wore a black silk evening dress which invited a sort of awed lust, while the jewellery which glittered about her head and breast seemed to be the pick of the finest pieces from Buccellati in Florence's Via Tornabuoni.

'I'm afraid I don't . . . ' Peroni let the sentence tail off, feeling embarrassed in his ignorance of the nobility.

'She gives parties,' said Marco coolly. 'At the last one the guests drew up champagne in silver buckets from the well in the courtyard of the Nicolini palace on the Grand Canal. I daresay she'll be overjoyed at the prospect of having you as a guest.'

Peroni couldn't repress a little smile of satisfaction.

As Marco had been talking, another guest had emerged from behind the latticework screen into their view. She must have been well over ninety years old and seemed to be the exclusive product of cosmeticians and dressmakers. Her delicately lifted face, as exquisitely painted as a Fragonard, moved a little jerkily as though pulled by invisible silk threads.

'Amata,' said Marco.

There was no need to say more. It was impossible not to have heard of Amata, the pen name under which the lady had achieved considerably more "novels for signorine", as they were known, than she had achieved years. It was said that she wrote one a week.

'Shall we start dinner?' called de Sanctis.

'That's my cue to be off,' said Marco to Peroni. 'Papa's dinner parties are brilliant affairs, but I find them a bit overpowering. I'm eating with friends.'

His exit was so neat and swift that he seemed suddenly to have become disembodied rather than simply to have gone. Briefly Peroni regretted the absence of this cheerful, irreverent young student.

Venice was sinking into a misty twilight as they sat down to a candlelit table in the centre of the terrace laid with arctic tablecloth and napkins, and crystal and cutlery that glittered as expensively as gems. Peroni was placed between the minister and the Contessa Guinzinelli, a heady combination for a man of his susceptibilities, for all that the lees of desolation lay thick at the bottom of his emotional cup.

The conversation was urbane and revolved flatteringly about Peroni. Everybody had heard of him; everybody wanted to know more of him. Particularly the minister who plied him with questions. The air was heavy with admiration.

'The extraordinary thing is,' interrupted Amata at a certain point in her lilting voice with its strong Tuscan accent, 'that I can't rid myself of the impression that I have created you, Commissario. You are my ideal hero. You are the personification of the Amata man, loved by millions of women throughout the world. Gallant, amusing, intensely good-looking with just a vein of mysterious melancholy . . .'

Almost against his will, Peroni found himself turning into the absurd women's magazine caricature of himself that Amata saw.

'As I look at you details of the plot keep floating into my mind, *as though I had already written it*! I see you dashing across the burning roof to save the heroine, smiling with aristocratic *hauteur* as the villain's pistol is pointed at your breast, lazily flicking the steering wheel of your Porsche as you pull out to overtake on the *autostrada* at two hundred kilometres an hour. And yet not a word of it has been written! Yet it shall be—I shall start it tomorrow! *Love and Blood*, I shall call it, "The passionate adventures of a police inspector".'

As they came to end of the fish *antipasto*, one fantasy Peroni was superimposed on another when Dino Dini presented a mimic portrayal of Peroni giving a television interview. It was a brilliant performance and caught him with such microscopic accuracy that Peroni recognised mannerisms in himself that he had hitherto been unaware of: a very slight jutting movement of the chin as he took in a question, the habit of fiddling with a ball-point as he talked, a just too frequent recourse to the phrase, 'You see what I mean?' Extraordinary, too, how the flabby rotundity of Dini could convey the impression of such elegant leanness.

When he had finished they applauded, and their applause awakened a couple of pigeons who were already installed for the night under the eaves of the roof. As the pigeons circled in brief alarm, Peroni had the impression that the applause was only in part for Dini, and principally for himself. De Sanctis and his guests were enthralled by the very idea of Peroni, even in a mirror.

Every so often the conversation would ebb a little away from him, only to flow back again from another direction shortly afterwards. The minister enquired with gratifying thoroughness into the details of his career. The Principessa Guinzinelli asked his opinions about politics and economy, and listened to the answers with masculine gravity. The Contessa Nicolini stimulated him into cadenzas of humour such as he had almost forgotten himself capable of.

And all the time de Sanctis sat at the head of the table, nodding and smiling with the air of a circus ringmaster who is well pleased with the way the performance is going. He was also, Peroni noticed, drinking heavily.

So the long, over abundant meal went on and only when it was at an end did Peroni realise, too late, that every seemingly harmless exchange he had taken part in, every smile he had evoked or bestowed, each mark of approval he had accepted had been like an invisible, weightless thread from a spider's web binding itself, unperceived by him, about his will. One of these threads he could have snapped, ten, perhaps even fifty. But not the great cord which had imperceptibly formed itself during that dinner.

He felt a sudden sense of dread.

The silence had been total for a space of time that was getting increasingly difficult to measure. De Sanctis stood motionless on the very edge of the two inner concentric circles with his hands raised, palms downwards, just above shoulder level. The others were grouped behind him.

Peroni, crippled by alcohol and by all the things which had been said and implied over dinner, stood apart, though safely within the outer circle, contemplating with impotent horror the change that had taken place in his fellow guests.

They had become sinister caricatures of themselves. The minister was a brooding hulk of political calculation, powered only by power. Amata was a waxwork infused with apparent life by an endless drip-feed of spiritual saccharine. Guinzinelli's rejected femininity seemed to have its own thwarted, anarchical growth within her like a cancer, while Nicolini's was like a monstrous rotting peach. Dini had become the personification of that braying, mindless laughter whose source is cruelty. As for de Sanctis he seemed a pitiless stone god.

And Peroni? What terrible transformation had he undergone?

The Commissario within was still on duty. Just. And he continued to insist that an end must be made now, whatever the cost.

But something else in Peroni, something that came from long dead generations of Neapolitan ancestors who had believed indiscriminately in anything that was supernatural just because it was supernatural—gods, demons, spirits, angels, the Tarot symbols, the luck that lived inside hunchbacks' humps—*that* something would not let him leave the protection of the circle. De Sanctis's words echoed hollowly in his mind.

'To stay outside can be dangerous.'

Twelve

Why did he wait so long to begin? Why did he always wait so long to begin? It was during this stage, the waiting stage when you had to stand there—silent, motionless and above all powerless to precipitate events—that she felt an impatience such as she had felt more than seventy-five years ago in the park of the old family villa outside Siena.

Porfirio had said that he would come for her at midnight in the summer house. She could still smell the heavy, commingled scents of the park on that summer night and hear the teeming, chaotic throb of the crickets as she waited in the hot dark.

She had needed Porfirio with painful urgency then as she now needed Them.

The ointments, the creams, the pills, the herbs, the elixirs with which all her houses were so copiously stocked; the masseuses and cosmeticians and specialised physicians with their animal gland treatments were all very well as far as they went. But when it came to the essence, the indispensable flow she was utterly dependent upon Them.

Porfirio had come. Extraordinarily handsome through the moonlight, with his heavy black moustaches, his square and martial chin, his tight braided uniform. And he had answered her urgency.

Porfirio had been the prototype of all her heroes. It mattered nothing that he had quickly proved to be stupid and cruel while they were generous, brave and tender; the fact was that it was into Porfirio's hard and rippling frame that she poured their tinselly virtues, so that pilot, explorer, playboy, millionaire, they were all reflections of him like an endless succession of mirrors all placed to catch the same image.

He had come that night, but would one of Them come tonight? They didn't always; sometimes they were capricious and even Fabrizio was incapable of summoning them. Then it was bad; she would retire to bed and lie there feeling the vital forces dripping out of her, concentrating all her will on surviving until next time.

That was rather how she felt now. It would be better if only he would start. Then at least there would be action—the feeling that at any moment one of Them might come.

If only he would start.

These long delays were particularly irritating because he knew they were calculated. He made similar delays himself before starting a speech, dragging them out as long they would hold to create maximum suspense, focus the listeners' attention, demonstrate his mastery.

As de Sanctis was doing now.

He had no doubt that the whole thing was a fraud. Much the same as politics in fact. The art of bamboozling the electorate, creating diversions, unleashing powerful emotions in others while keeping your own under strict control. Quackery.

Why then did he come? Because there were powerful contacts to be made that way, because the network of this secret society stretched throughout Italy, throughout the western world, and in all the highest places at least one person was involved. Because like all secret societies it furthered the power and wealth of its members.

Was that all, Minister?

Of course it was all.

Then what about that charging of inner power, that surging of energy, that sense of mastership and absolute self-confidence that came each time? That came from something outside himself. From some One outside himself.

Cleverly induced self-deception. The same as the righteous indignation, the enthusiasms, the fears and all the other emotions which he could induce in the electorate.

And yet knowing all this quite well, it was with a tightening of excitement in his ample belly that the minister perceived de

93

Sanctis was about to begin.

'*Dies mies jeschet boenedoesef douvema enitemaus.*'

It was no language Peroni had ever heard, and in the *Questura* with the passing of time one did get to hear a surprising variety of languages. Probably just gibberish. And yet he had the odd impression that de Sanctis intended it for comprehension by someone. But who? One of their circle? Or someone, some presence outside it?

Peroni checked his racing Neapolitan fancy. Just before de Sanctis had started to intone he had come to a resolution. He would stay. Not for social or any other advancement, but because this rite was part of the investigation. Kehzia was dead and all this may well have had something to do with her death.

So he would stay. Without allowing himself to be drawn in. Above all without allowing himself to believe.

For there was nothing to believe in.

There was this man, see, got this job as a barkeep in a wild west town. 'Just remember,' they says to him, 'when you hear that Terrible Tom's coming—get out of town, fast!' Well, everything goes OK for some while until one day he hears a great shout—'Terrible Tom's coming to town!' So there's a great big rush, see, to get out and in the rush this barkeep gets knocked over unconscious. When he comes to there's a man standing over him, three metres tall, blood red eyes, shoulders like a bull, breathing fire and holding a whip of live rattlesnakes.

'Whisky!' says the man.

So the barkeep gives him a bottle and he bites off the neck and swallows the whole bottle in one.

'You want another?' says the barkeep.

'No,' says the man, 'I can't wait now—Terrible Tom's coming to town!'

It was a bit like that each time. Or each time de Sanctis succeeded in calling one of Them up. You thought you were going to be swallowed up by the worst power of all, only to find out that there was a still more Terrible Tom to come.

94

And the legions of them were infinite.

So why did he come? Because it was the only kick left. Show business—his braying chasm of a laugh which audiences found so infectious—had given him all the others: fame for a start, sex in all its varieties, fast cars, luxury travel. True, he had to enjoy them all through his flabby, disgusting body, the only means he had of conveying kicks to himself. But that he had learned to live with, and the kicks came hard and rapid.

The trouble had begun when they started making themselves less violently felt; at first just perceptibly less, then much less and finally with a catastrophic diminution of intensity, until the most violent, the most unusual, the most exotic of kicks reached him as though he were wadded against it by several tons of cotton wool.

Then he had met Fabrizio de Sanctis and, through his agency, Them. And the kicks had started again. They came with a difference now, though, for they came with fear. Fear each time of Terrible Tom.

Or rather, he sometimes thought, it was like those Russian dolls which contain within themselves an exact replica of themselves, and the replica in turn contains within itself another exact replica of itself, and so on. The difference being that the Terrible Toms got bigger each time. And what scared Dino Dini was that one day he would meet up with the biggest of them all, and then there would be no Dino Dini left to exasperate into laughter an Italy in which even the initials of the biggest state travel agency, CIT, stand for corruption, inflation and terrorism. All that would be left would be one unimaginably colossal Terrible Tom licking its lips on one infinitesimal fraction of humanity.

But in the meantime it was like playing Russian roulette; the alternating periods of suspense and relief were heart beats which stopped him from dying of boredom.

'*Dies mies jeschet boenedosef douvema enitemaus.*'

The invocation was repeated, and fear of Terrible Tom crept about Dino Dini's heart like water rising in a lock.

The Principessa Guinzinelli was in it literally for the money.

Money was the only thing she cared for on this earth; she worshipped it with pure and unwavering fervour and she could never make enough of it. Until one day she had heard that the kingdom of Hell was able and sometimes willing to distribute wealth unlimited to its subjects.

She went into the business with the same precision and thoroughness that she gave to any other deal. She studied the subject in all its aspects, she weighed the pros and cons, she hired experts, she put out feelers, she parleyed, she bargained, she asked for samples. Then she made up her mind and signed her contract with the powers of darkness.

And so far the terms had been scrupulously observed.

The profit curve of her stores had started to shift upwards, at first only slightly, like the uncertain stirrings of an upturned glass when everybody's fingers are rested upon it at the outset of a session. Was somebody pushing? Was it only a natural phenomenon? Or was there some other reason for the movement? And then the tendency became more decisive, like the glass when it makes purposefully for the letters. Up and up the profits had continued to climb until they began to occupy an increasingly larger place in the financial pages of the newspapers.

Sometimes the Principessa doubted. When you believe only in money you have little faith left over for the supernatural, even when it is that very supernatural which is providing you with the money. Might it be no more than her own financial skill which was universally considered outstanding? Might it be no more than coincidence that the upward curve had started at the same time as she had made her pact with the Others? Might it also be coincidence that the occasional downward fluctuations in the stores' balance sheets always came after de Sanctis had failed to summon one of Them? It might. But the Principessa Guinzinelli did not intend to put it to the test by abandoning the cult.

Besides she felt curiously at home in their company. Women she disliked and despised (and never more so than when they were satisfying her physical need of them); men she disliked and secretly envied. But the sheer, unphysical being of Them answered some call in the deepest and most unexplored regions of herself.

Always assuming that They existed.

'*Dies mies jeschet boenedosef douvema enitemaus.*'

It was the third call. Was there to be no answer tonight?

All these people—the minister, the old hag who wrote those drivelling books, that fat and vulgar comedian, the lesbian Guinzinelli—were converts to Satanism. Just how firm was the faith of each individual was impossible to say, but one thing they all shared was the self-conscious, slightly strained intensity of the convert.

The Contessa Nicolini was what you might call a cradle Satanist. The cult had been in her family for generations and, coming to her as it did along with the family name and traditions, she had always taken it quite naturally. She knew the demonic hierarchy rather as the Roman aristocracy might know the heavenly one, and like them she felt the same easy familiarity with it. Awe, worship, fear were for the common people and the converts. For her there was only meticulously concealed boredom.

Not that she would have dreamed of abandoning the cult; it was part of one's life, part of one's duty and she went through the motions as her ancestors had done. It was all a bit like the British royal family attending some particularly tedious official function; one smiled, one showed one's approval, one sat through it, one did one's job. But fundamentally one remained quite indifferent.

Oh, things happened all right; she had seen them and heard them many times. But to what could they be ascribed? To Beelzebub, Lucifer, Moloch, Astaroth and all the rest of them? To de Sanctis himself? To someone else not in this room at all at the moment? To the greedy imaginations of the converts? Or to those aimless combinations of circumstances which form galaxies and cancers? The Contessa Nicolini really didn't know and didn't expect to know either.

In the meantime whatever the causation might be, it was singularly absent tonight. De Sanctis had scrupulously ob-

97

served all the ritual and had uttered the formula of evocation three times without anything happening.

And then, loudly, a dog barked.

Thirteen

And then, loudly, a dog barked.

Peroni started at the sound of it and looked bewilderedly about in the half light. It had been a single rumbling bark, but with no joy of welcome in it; rather it had been a growl accompanied by a baring of teeth to rip through flesh.

It seemed to come from within the room itself, and yet there was no sign of a dog now, nor had been all the evening. And surely no dog, however big or aggressive, could have made its voice heard so clearly from outside?

Peroni's acquaintance with the supernatural was instinctive rather than knowledgeable, but he seemed to have heard or read that the malign powers often made their presences felt with a manifold variety of signs and sounds.

So why not the barking of a dog?

The idea was absurd, thought the Commissario. He had decided to stay as part of the investigation into Kehzia Michaelis's disappearance. Without allowing himself to be drawn in. Or to believe. Those had been the terms and they must be respected.

So it was almost entirely instinctively that Peroni took a step further into the protection of the sword-traced circle.

Amata's ancient frame thrilled at the sound. They were coming after all. Or One of Them was. He had announced His presence and would not now withdraw.

For a moment the sensation of excitement mixed with relief was almost unbearable. She was assured another lease of vitality, of sparkling eyes and perfect complexion.

The head of the nearly centenarian novelist was jerked in the direction of the barking sound, and in the semi-darkness you could almost have mistaken the smile upon her lips as the same smile with which she had welcomed Porfirio outside the summer house more than three-quarters of a century before.

Terrible Tom was coming. Dino Dini tensed himself for the encounter, his shambling, repulsive frame behind the back of Fabrizio de Sanctis. De Sanctis represented protection, in theory at any rate; he was supposed to be able to dominate the spirits he called up; and indeed so long as it was a question of the lower ranks of demons Dini supposed this might well be so. So long as it was demons like the star-shaped Buer who teaches philosophy, logic and the virtues of medicinal herbs; or the stupid, elephant-formed Biemot whose strength is in his kidneys and whom most demonologists identify with the wine steward of Hell; or the simple-minded Ukobach of the lean and scalded body, generally held to be the inventor of fried foods and fireworks—so long as it was one of these, de Sanctis could surely control them.

But when it came to the mightier power—Gap, Grand President and Prince of Hell with sixty legions at his command; or Paimone, one of the Kings of the lower regions, a member of the angelic orders and the Powers, and master of two hundred legions; or Lucifer with the form of a lovely boy who some believed to be Satan himself; or come to that the one de Sanctis was evoking now—when it came to these might not his authority suddenly crack?

And what would become of Dino Dini then?

It was all trickery, of course. That barking noise for instance which seemed to come from the middle of the room: a carefully concealed tape-recorder. In all the months he had attended these rituals there had not been a single effect which he had not been able to ascribe to material causes. Well, perhaps just one or two had been a little hard to analyze, but that merely meant that de Sanctis knew his job.

Come to think of it, conjuring could well be exploited in politics. Imagine the effect that could be created on the voters with certain carefully selected tricks during election addresses.

100

One would have to be careful, of course, because if the Communists got onto it they would expose it mercilessly and keep the scandal at boiling point for a very long time.

But it would certainly bear consideration . . .

At least something was happening. To say that the Principessa Guinzinelli relied on the infernal powers for her profits, as Hitler relied on his astrologers, would be untrue; she was too independent and had too high an opinion of her own powers. Nevertheless, she had felt a slight relaxation of tension at the sound of that single, menacing bark. The process was underway.

And then she heard something else. A slow, breathing sound which gathered in volume until it became almost a roar; then, just as it seemed about to engulf them, it started to decrescendo down to a breath again. And then the crescendo began once more and so on, like a wave gathering strength as it massed towards the shore, breaking and then receding.

The Principessa felt the urge for a cigar.

The Contessa Nicolini was a mistress at keeping up appearances. This evening, as on every other evening of her life, she had consumed a large amount of alcohol, but to look at her you never would have said so.

Equally now to look at her you would have said she was wholly and devoutly taken up with the ritual about her and you would never have noticed that she was observing the converts with detached curiosity.

Converts fell into two categories: those who believed and those who doubted, or at any rate vaunted themselves on doubting. Both categories were represented this evening.

Those who took pride in what they called doubt were the bigger fools, but the believers were fools too because, in belief, they submitted themselves to fear, greed or imbecility. In any case to servitude.

But what about that extraordinarily good-looking southern policeman? He didn't pride himself on disbelieving because with part of himself he believed, and yet he was not servile in

101

belief. So much she understood, and yet he remained a puzzle to her.

Exactly what, for instance, was he making of the waves as they broke against the walls of the room?

How could there be waves breaking against the walls of the room? That Venice was due to be engulfed in the sea Peroni was aware, but surely not so suddenly?

He looked at de Sanctis. The man was standing with his hands raised in the air as though he were commanding the waves, and Peroni was reminded of a picture he had once seen of Moses dividing the Red Sea. The awesome power of water leashed. But this was a diabolical Moses commanding diabolical waves. No children of Israel would pass through these waves to a promised land, but rather the children of Hell would be engulfed by them. And Peroni in their company.

'*Stronzo!*' the Commissario barked mutely at the other, fantastical Peroni. But the very use of the obscenity showed that he was feeling the strain. 'Suggestion,' he insisted, 'pure suggestion.'

Suggestion? Maybe that would explain it better than trickery, thought the minister. It would be hard for a recording machine, even with the most expensive stereo equipment, to make the sound of waves appear to be coming from outside and all about them.

Suggestion then. But was the same suggestion acting upon the others? For the first time the minister wondered whether the observable phenomena at the rituals might differ from person to person.

Either way, the art behind it was consummate. He wished that he might be empowered with such art, and even as he wished it something seemed to tell him that he might be . . .

Perhaps you might be, thought the Contessa Nicolini. Perhaps you might be able to devour him. Already he had smelled her, like a dog smelling a bitch on heat, and that was very satisfactory. But he still had a measure of dignity, idealism, and

102

while those remained she could not devour him.

What she needed was power. Power to enslave, degrade and finally utterly absorb the southern policeman into herself. And whatever one's attitude towards the cult, however one might despise the converts, one had to admit that it could confer power.

She felt herself being invested with power . . .

She felt herself being invested with power. It was her own power to transform human lives, emotions, passions, eventually everything about her into money. Her own power, and yet somehow connected with the waves that were rushing all about them, intermingled now with the sound of barking, fiercer and louder than before.

She could feel that It was coming . . .

She could feel that It was coming. Bearing down upon her as Porfirio had borne down upon her, bringing with It eternal youth, the perfect complexion of a girl, the power to be eternally feminine and to communicate eternal femininity to millions of readers.

The wonderful Thing was coming. The terrible Thing was coming . . .

Terrible Tom was coming. This time it really would be Him. This time when the barkeep said, 'Do you want another?' there would be no merciful punch-line once again postponing the final kick of all until next time.

This time there would be devouring . . .

This time there would be devouring. She had reached the point where other lovers merely tormented her appetite as crumbs would torment a starving man. But this one would satisfy her. For a while.

There was another sound now mixed in with the waves and the barking. It sounded like the roaring of oxen. She heard it and she did not hear it . . .

He heard it and he did not hear it. The Contessa Nicolini with her black evening dress and her jewellery flashing as though it emitted its own light was standing a few feet away from him, and yet he felt as though he were being sucked towards her.

Towards her and into her. You didn't have to go into space to find non-existence in a black hole.

He was overwhelmed by the roaring of oxen and the breaking of waves and the barking of a dog . . .

And the barking of a dog was endless wealth and the roaring of oxen . . .

And the roaring of oxen was power and the breaking of waves . . .

And the breaking of waves was eternal youth and the barking of a dog . . .

And the barking of a dog was Terrible Tom and the roaring of oxen . . .

And the roaring of oxen was the orgasm of the man called Peroni being sucked inside her and the breaking of waves . . .

And suddenly there was silence and Peroni found himself, by what power he could not tell, to be still himself. And everything seemed to have returned to within hailing distance of normality, if you could overlook pentagrams, magic circles, skulls and the other macabre oddities.

But it was only a seeming return, for there was something horribly Abnormal now present in the room. Something far more horribly so than the previous grotesque sound effects. Yet the curious thing was that there was nothing that could be perceived by the senses. Nothing except de Sanctis, his arms still raised in invocation, and Peroni's fellow guests.

And then as he looked at them he saw that they were all staring at the same point: the innermost of the three concentric circles in which nobody had set foot and which was now, as it had been all along, empty.

But it wasn't empty.

Standing within it was a monstrous bird. A blackbird, but far bigger than any blackbird Peroni had ever seen and with an air of insolent, somehow obscene authority which demanded absolute subservience.

Demanded it and got it. One by one, starting with the ancient novelist and the comedian and ending with the Contessa Nicolini, the worshippers sank down till their arms and legs were outstretched and their faces were pressed against the floor.

Only Peroni and de Sanctis remained standing. It seemed to Peroni as though the bird's right eye (the left belonged to that side of its profile which was turned away from him and which he never saw) was staring at him and then into him, observing the most secret parts of his hidden self, recognising the falsity of the Commissario, recognising the *scugnizzo* not so much for what he was as for what he could become.

In that single black and glittering eye was the reflection of the truly evil Peroni of whom the *scugnizzo* was mere potential. That was the person he could so easily become and that was the person this nightmare bird recognised and claimed as its rightful subject.

Peroni stared with a mixture of awe and horror at his infernal self and then, after an incalculable time when the sight had become unbearable, closed his eyes against it.

When he opened them again both his other self and the giant blackbird in whose eye it had been reflected had vanished.

Fourteen

By tilting the hand-shaker you could roll a silver ball up a sort of plastic mound with a hole in the top of it like the crater in a volcano. If you rolled too slow the ball wouldn't make it to the top; if you rolled too fast it skidded over the hole and down the other side. Only if you took it at exactly the correct speed and angle, like a rocket re-entering the earth's atmosphere, would the ball be caught in the crater at the top.

De Sanctis plainly wasn't concentrating on the game, however. He manipulated it absently every now and then with his left hand while in his right he held a chunky crystal glass of Chivas Regal, a bottle of which he was sharing with Peroni. The bottle was nearly empty and it was not the first.

Peroni badly wanted to find out exactly what was being offered him now, and why, but for some reason he was quite powerless to accelerate the course of events. It was as though he and de Sanctis were playing some sort of game the progress of which was regulated by an invisible third party. The blackbird?

'How did you do it?' said Peroni, enunciating carefully for fear of slurring.

Instead of answering de Sanctis went over and drew open the curtains of one of the windows. It was still dark outside, but in the eastern sky over Venice there was a faint tinging of grey which suggested that dawn was not far off.

When the ritual had been concluded and the guests had taken their leave Peroni, as though by implicit agreement, had remained behind with de Sanctis, but neither of them had referred to the issues that lay between them like droppings of the giant blackbird. Peroni's question was the first attempt to open serious negotiations.

'How did I do what?' said de Sanctis at last, a polite

expression on his Grecian face which seemed to suggest that the question was in slightly dubious taste.

'The bird,' said Peroni, ignoring the suggestion, 'The barking and the rest of the noises.'

'Do you really believe, Commissario, that I *did* something?'

'Of course.' But Peroni was by no means so sure as the Commissario sounded.

Putting down whisky and hand-shaker, de Sanctis went over to the bookcase from which he returned with a large, leather-bound book. It looked something like an old and very expensive atlas. This he opened at a page and handed to Peroni who turned the book over first and looked at the title. *Dictionnaire Infernal*, it said, ascribing the authorship to a certain J. Collin de Plancy.

Not greatly the wiser, Peroni went back to the two pages indicated by de Sanctis and was shocked to see a portrait of the giant blackbird that was so exact as to seem almost a reflection. The bird was even in the same stance, showing its right profile with a single black and beady eye staring up at Peroni out of the page.

For a second he stared at it, trying to give no sign of the superstitious awe which spluttered and flared about the minia-ture, private Naples he carried in his head. Then he looked at the opposite page. Less than half of it was printed: three brief paragraphs and a heading in some exotically baroque type-face.

CAYM said the heading, and Peroni recognised the letters which de Sanctis had traced with charcoal between the two inner concentric circles. The text was in French which he read with no difficulty.

Demon of superior class, it said, *Grand President of the Infernal Regions.*

Usually appears in the guise of a blackbird. Is said to be the most skilled sophist in Hell. With the astuteness of his arguments he can topple the most precisely constructed logic. It was with him that Luther had the famous dispute of which he conserved the record for us.

Caym gives understanding of the roaring of oxen, the barking of dogs and the sound of the waves. He can read the future. This

107

demon, who formerly belonged to the angelic hosts, today commands thirty legions in Hell.

Tumult threatened a *coup d'état* in Peroni's inner Naples.

'Are you suggesting,' he said, 'that this is the bird you conjured up earlier this evening?'

In de Sanctis's left hand the silver ball rolled up the mound, checked just below the mouth of the crater and rolled back again. Too slow.

'You saw what you saw,' he said, 'Now I have given you the key to interpret it.'

'You *believe* this?' said Peroni, 'You believe in devils?'

'You don't?' said de Sanctis.

It was at this exact moment that Peroni first became consciously aware of something that must have been going on for some little while. Beneath his flamboyant Pucci tie he wore a medal bearing the image of St Janarius, the patron saint of Naples whose blood still miraculously liquefies three times a year in the cathedral of Naples to the clamorous enthusiasm of the Neapolitans. St Janarius, it was said, never says no, not even to the most reprehensible Neapolitans. Peroni's faith in general was perhaps neither as limpid nor as fervent as it might have been, but in his devotion to St Janarius he had always remained unswerving. And over the years St Janarius had never let Peroni down. On many occasions when his chances of survival had appeared to be about as good as those of somebody who has just jumped from the top of the leaning tower of Pisa he had invoked the former bishop of Naples. And invariably something had occurred which allowed him to go on living. There was never anything about these events which prevented you from putting them down to coincidence. But, in spite of the often sceptical observations of the Commissario, Peroni never did.

And now he realised that the little medal around his neck was glowing, and had been doing so for some little while.

Although, of course, the impression of glowing could perfectly well have been generated by his own body heat.

'If you give it a moment's thought,' de Sanctis was saying, 'it becomes obvious that only the most superficial of thinkers can

disbelieve in devils. Locke and Newton accepted their existence.
So did Clarke and Leibniz.'

Reliable witnesses presumably.

'Pope Paul VI,' de Sanctis went on, 'no mean intelligence,
was quite unequivocal about it. One of the principal needs of
the Church today, he said—and I quote—"is the defence
against that evil which we call the Devil. Evil is not merely a
deficiency, but an efficiency, a living being, spiritual, perverted
and perverting. A dreadful reality. Mysterious and terrifying."
Not perhaps quite my choice of vocabulary throughout, but
there can be no question about the substance.'

Peroni was shaken. Then an objection occurred to him. 'I'm
not denying the Devil's existence,' he said, feeling this was big of
him, 'but from that, in the singular, to—'

'To Caym?'

'Exactly.'

'If you'll forgive me, Commissario, your theology—or more
exactly your demonology—is weak. Accounts vary as to what
actually happened at the beginning of creation, but according
to the most widely held version the demons, emphatically in the
plural, were all part of the angelic host. Then at a certain point
which the Jewish rabbi Aben-Esra traces to the second day of
creation a number of these angels had the stupendous independence and originality of spirit to rebel against the very order of
creation itself. Satan, first among the cherubim, put himself at
the head of the rebels. But they were defeated and precipitated
from Paradise. General opinion has named their destination as
Hell, but not all authorities have agreed about this. St Paul
speaks of demons of the air. St Prospero believed that they lived
in fogs and mists. Swinden sustained that their dwelling is the
sun. But all serious students hold that there is a large number of
them. Wierus says that they are divided into six thousand six
hundred and sixty six legions each one containing the same
number of demons. That would give us a total of approximately
forty-five million. And each one with his own marked idiosyn-
cracies, for rebellion always indicated originality of nature.'

De Sanctis suddenly tilted the hand-shaker and the silver ball
shot up the mound and over the crater. Too fast. 'In view of

that,' he said, 'does not Caym seem—a little less improbable?'

'In theory perhaps.'

'But not in practice?'

'Why should I be concerned with practice?'

'Perhaps you're already more concerned with practice than you imagine.'

Peroni felt the sensation that he normally associated with the realisation that he was being watched. 'What do you mean?' he said.

'Let me reply with another question, Commissario. Assuming these demons to exist, what do you imagine they do?'

'They tempt,' said Peroni. The question and answer form made him think of a black catechism.

'Yes, they tempt,' said de Sanctis with the partial approval of an instructor whose pupil has given a correct, but insufficient answer, 'They tempt those who are too obtuse to recognise their existence and those who are so self-righteous as to consider themselves part of the opposition. Put together these form the vast majority. But there is a small minority who recognise the existence of demons and, far from opposing them, assist them. What do you think is the activity of the demons in regard to this minority?'

'I have no idea.'

'They *give!*' said de Sanctis. He tilted his hand-shaker for the third time and this time the silver ball rolled up the mound at exactly the right speed and angle so that it settled with QED finality into the crater.

For the first time Peroni realised with clarity what the destination was he had been heading for all that evening. Or maybe all his life. The glowing on his chest was more marked. Now was the time to get out.

'What do they give?' The voice seemed not to be his own and, although he had tried to rise, something had held him back in his chair. Whisky maybe. Or the black wings of a gigantic bird. 'What do they give?'

'Everything that's worth having.'

'Easily said.'

'There's authority for it. In his account of a certain temptation, the Greek writer, Luke, quotes the Devil as saying, "All this power will I give thee, and the glory of them: for that is delivered unto me; and to whomsoever I will I give it." To *whomsoever I will*, Commissario!'

'There doesn't seem to be much evidence of demonic generosity,' said Peroni, 'looking back over the past.'

'How do you know?' said de Sanctis. 'Because of the stupidity of the vast majority of people, adherence to Satan has almost invariably had to be a secret. So it is quite possible that every single rich, powerful and famous person throughout the history of mankind has been a secret worshipper of Satan. To whomsoever I will I give it.'

Peroni thought of one or two rich, powerful and famous people he had met and saw no reason to doubt the logic of it.

'The minister,' said de Sanctis, apparently changing the subject, 'a pleasant man.'

'So far as I could tell.'

'He certainly likes you.'

'Oh?'

'He mentioned to me that he thought you were being wasted. He said that your talents would be better employed in a top police job in Rome.'

Peroni felt a gust of unholy glee. This was something everybody in Italy dreamed of: a minister to reach down into the struggling mass of humanity and pick you out of it to set you on a pinnacle.

'The Principessa Guinzinelli,' de Sanctis went on, 'was most interested when she heard of you. Apparently her stores have a considerable security problem and she hoped you might be able to devise an original scheme for overcoming it. The fee would be extremely high, and the job would lead to others.'

Money. Throughout his life Peroni had suffered from the shortage of it. It was as though he had never managed to catch up after the extreme poverty of his *scugnizzo* days. And now he was being offered unlimited wealth. Cases of Chivas Regal whisky, clothes from Mayfair, a flat in Piazza Navona and a villa in the hills outside Rome. His head swam at the prospect.

'Oh, and this,' said de Sanctis handing him an envelope. 'A

111

token of good things to come.'

Peroni opened the envelope. Inside was an invitation card which looked as though it might have been for a presidential reception. Beneath a gold embossed crest was written, *The Contessa Nicolini requests the presence of Commissario Achille Peroni to a banquet to be held on 7th October at the Villa dei Giganti, Lugano in honour of the visit of HRH Vittorio Emanuele di Savoia.*

Peroni was a republican, but as a Neapolitan he had an inbred love of the very idea of monarchy and this, unexpressed and unrecognised for the best part of his life, now burst into instant flower.

'*Buona sera*, Commissario,' he imagined the lean and balding heir to the house of Savoy saying to him, "I have followed your career with interest."

'Your Highness is very kind . . . '

The imaginary dialogue was interrupted by de Sanctis. 'To say that something is expected of you in exchange for these and all the other benefits to come would be false. Nothing so mundane as bargaining is envisaged. But as always when somebody adheres to a society a small token gesture is expected.'

His soul! That was what it was all about. Even at the peak of this high mountain he felt more than a qualm at the prospect, and the glowing of the medal was now almost painful.

'What has St Janarius ever given you?' said a voice, and it was hard to tell whether it came from within or without, 'Has St Janarius ever invited you to meet Vittorio Emanuele at a banquet? Or to devise a highly paid security scheme for the Guinzinelli stores throughout Italy? Has St Janarius ever obtained a top post for you in Rome?'

Something flickered in Peroni's mind recalling the number of times his life had been saved following frantic SOS calls to the patron saint of Naples.

'Coincidence,' said the voice, 'Coincidence and your own cleverness.'

All the same, his soul . . .

'A very small token gesture indeed, I think you'll agree,' de

112

Sanctis went on. 'To show your good will you would be asked temporarily to suspend your enquiries at Jesolo.'

Not his soul. Yet the medal of St Janarius, continuing to glow upon his skin, said that it was merely another way of saying his soul.

'Why?' he said, evading the main issue.

'Part of the bargain is that no questions should be asked.'

Another objection occurred to him. 'I can hardly abandon an enquiry,' he said, 'without questions being asked at the *Questura*.'

'Don't worry about that,' said de Sanctis. 'Tonight you met five other members of our network, but there are many others. Everywhere. Including the *Questura*.'

'And if I refuse?'

De Sanctis looked at the prospect as though it were an impossible bet on a gambling table, then he upturned his palms with an urbane expression. 'Then you refuse,' he said.

But no jobs in Rome, no parleying with Vittorio Emanuele, no contracts with the Principessa Guinzinelli.

'Very well,' said Peroni, 'I accept.'

Shortly afterwards as Peroni was going by motorboat along the deserted, dawn-stirring canals towards his apartment near the Rialto he could still feel the medal of St Janarius glowing on his chest.

He undid the top button of his shirt, ripped off the medal and threw it into the canal.

St Janarius

Fifteen

'You wouldn't think with legs like that she'd wear Bermudas at all, would you *angelo mio*? But they never learn. You might almost say they dress to emphasize their worst points. Look at this one now—English I should say. A neck like an old rooster, tits like pricked balloons and she has to wear a dress open down to her belly.'

It was a slack moment in the shop and, as he often did on such occasions, Benito Mussolini was going through the photographs which were ready for collection and passing them on to Desdemona. She took them as he handed them to her, studied them gravely for a second or so and then either bared her long teeth and pinks gums in derisive laughter or expressed in a high-pitched chatter what sounded like her moral indignation.

'How old would you say this one was, *tesoro*? Thirteen? Maybe not even that. And look what she's wearing! You can see everything she's got underneath! There ought to be a law against it—it's that sort of thing that causes crime, you know.'

Benito Mussolini had a pronounced streak of puritanism which it seemed that Desdemona shared for, as he passed her the photograph of the scarcely teenage girl, the monkey broke out into a chatter of furious outrage.

It was while she was thus expressing her opinion of feminine immodesty that her master happened to look out through the shop window. As he did so his mouth fell open with the remains of a cigarette attached to the lower lip. He stared, blinked and stared again until there could no longer be any doubt.

'Wait for me here, *stella*,' he said. 'I'll be back in a few minutes.'

And having hung the *Vengo Subito* on the shop door, he locked up and crossed the road.

117

Following somebody in Jesolo during the season is no great problem for there are always people about to provide you with cover. In fact, the danger is that you may lose your quarry, for there are so many side turnings and entrances to shops and hotels, *pensioni* and parking lots that they may easily slip away without your noticing. And Benito didn't want that to happen, for by the purest chance he had spotted one of the two people who had been in the photograph with the missing Michaelis girl.

But as it was now mid-September the crowd was noticeably thinner than it had been a month before and Benito was able to keep the person in view without particular difficulty.

As he went he thought hard. Where was the person going? To a hotel it was to be hoped, for Benito knew all the lobby clerks in Jesolo and there would be no problem in getting all the particulars he needed. A *pensione* would be almost as easy. Flats might prove more troublesome.

And then? When he had the particulars, what was the next step?

We'll worry about that when we come to it, he told himself; this was a game to be played strictly move by move.

Past the Lorelei Hotel; past the games arcade throbbing to the sound of electronic cops and robbers; past Peter's Pub offering its customers Best Beer, Irish Coffee, Fish and Chips, Baked Beans on Toast; past the Neptune Hotel, *Zimmer frei, Schwimmbad*; past Irene, *Parucchiera per Signore* with several wigs on polystyrene skulls in the window and a notice offering lessons in all scholastic subjects; past a board announcing cinema showings of Robin Hood and, *Deutscher Sprach*, Super Porn.

Where were they going?

And then, with Benito Mussolini's bubble of perplexity near bursting point, the quarry turned off Via Verdi down one of the many side streets. This would make following unobserved more difficult, but not greatly so.

And anyway shortly after that the destination was reached, but at the very last minute there was an awkward surprise, for the quarry turned briefly and Benito Mussolini had the impression he had been recognised.

Light reached him heavily filtered and brought with it a sense of
dread for the imminent awakening. He was in some way
imprisoned and, moving to discover the nature of his imprisonment, found that it was the sheet over his head.

But when he removed this he found that the events of the
previous night were hovering, vulture-like, outside and now
they pounced upon him. Horror was topped up with remorse
when he felt an emptiness about his neck and remembered the
medal which had finished at the bottom of the canal.

St Janarius never says no. St Janarius does not withdraw his
aid even, or indeed particularly, from the dregs of Neapolitan
society, but those dregs have to be at least nominally on the
same side. And now Peroni had ranged himself, knowingly and
wilfully, with the enemy.

He had abandoned St Janarius and St Janarius had no
alternative but to abandon him.

His first reaction was to wonder how this state of affairs could
be reversed, but then he caught a glimpse in the high, ornate,
but cracked mirror—one of the many eccentric furnishing of
Peroni's Rialto apartment— of that new self he had last seen
reflected in the bright and evil eye of the monstrous blackbird.
And he began to feel a grudging admiration for it.

And then he began to think of the rewards. The banquet in
Lugano. The job in Rome. The contract with the Principessa
Guinzinelli. But why? The question blocked his exultation.
Even those massive bribes could not anaesthetise Peroni's
questing curiosity. Why should they want him to suspend his
enquiries at Jesolo? Did they want to prevent him finding out
more about Kehzia's disappearance? Or was there some other
reason? And if so what?

But as de Sanctis had stipulated there should be no questions,
Peroni determined to slaughter his curiosity and, if it wouldn't
be slaughtered, then at least keep it in hiding.

So, quarter of an hour later, with this resolution firmly
adopted it was no longer a wretchedly divided Peroni who
walked out through the front door of the flaking, damp and

ancient *palazzo* and set off for the bar at the end of the *calle*. It was no longer a more or less scrupulous police officer with a secret Neapolitan alter ego.

It was an all evil Peroni.

'No sign of *dott*. Peroni?' asked Roberti.

'No,' said Perez who had come into Jesolo that morning, 'and he hasn't been into the *Questura* at Venice, either—I've just telephoned.'

'Maybe he's ill,' suggested Roberti.

'Maybe he's with a woman,' said Perez.

Inwardly Roberti was shocked at this; outwardly he did his best to look unconcerned.

'Anyway, we'd better be getting on with things,' said Perez. 'Just take a look at this interview he had with the American yesterday.'

Roberti read it. 'We'd better get onto the other people at the party,' he said when he had finished.

'Just so. And see if we can get a line on the one like a boxer. Tell you what, why don't you go over there and see them. You can have *baccalà alla vicentina* for lunch on expenses.'

'Right, *dottore*.'

'And while you're doing that I'll see if I can get a line onto this Cheea who might have been Kehzia. If she's dead there must be a body somewhere. In fact,' he went on after a pause, 'we could do with a bit more information all round about Cheea-who-might-have-been-Kehzia.'

'So what about that, *stella mia*? A bit of a surprise, wouldn't you say? But the awkward thing is, there were two of them with her in the photograph. So it might have been the other one that got rid of her. What do you say to that?'

Desdemona considered the point and then chattered subduedly.

'You have a point there, *tesoro*,' said Benito when she had done. 'Maybe it was both of them together that got rid of her. But even so the one that we're onto will be interested in getting hold of the photograph, no?'

Desdemona apparently agreed.

'So either way what they call an exploratory discussion won't come amiss, will it? Oh, by the way,' he went on after an instant's reflection, 'I've got an idea that maybe I was recognised.'

The monkey chattered interrogatively.

"No, no, *fiore mio*—I don't mean there's any relationship between us. But we're public figures in Jesolo, you and I—lots of people know *us* without us having the slightest idea who *they* are. That's the sort of recognition I mean. Do you think it might be dangerous?'

Desdemona made more dubious noises.

'Maybe you're right, *amore*, maybe you're right,' said Benito. 'So we'll have to play this very carefully indeed. I'll tell you what—we won't make any appointments that aren't in a public place with lots of people about. After all, we can't come to any great harm in the middle of Jesolo, can we?'

Desdemona made more dubious noises.

'Don't you worry your pretty little head about me, *bellissima*,' said Benito patting her. 'I'll look after myself. I've been looking after myself pretty well up to now, haven't I?'

He picked up the telephone receiver.

But how to pass the time?

In the full knowledge that the price would be even heavier in the end, Peroni had chased off the hangover that swirled like storm clouds in his head with another considerable intake of Chivas Regal.

That done he went to the *Questura*. Whether it was a coincidence or not he couldn't tell, but nobody asked any awkward questions; indeed, nobody said anything, almost as though the word had gone out that he was not to be harrassed.

So it was true somebody at the *Questura* was one of them. But who? Peroni considered his colleagues and particularly his superiors in this new light. Or rather this new darkness. Ostensibly they were all more or less prosaic, common-sensical and conscientious policemen. So who would believe that one or more of them worshipped Satan and took his hand-outs?

Come to that who would have believed it of Peroni himself? He sat undisturbed in his office overlooking the Fondementa San Lorenzo. The view from his window, with the canal stirring almost imperceptibly in its bed, made it seem that a Sleeping Beauty spell had been cast upon Venice.

How to pass the time?

There were more than a dozen things to be done, but none that stirred him from his lethargy. His existence in Venice was that of a glorified hotel detective, and then the hunt for Kehzia had taken him into the brash, loud world of Jesolo and given him a real problem to be involved with. A person to be involved with.

Peroni recognised that his thoughts were going in a direction inimical to his new existence, and he switched them once again to the rewards that were coming to him. Prospects were glowing, he told himself, prospects had never glowed so much before.

It would soon pass, this feeling of utter desolation which even the whisky could not drown.

Apathetically he noticed that the Sleeping Beauty scene outside his window had been enlivened. Not by movement, however, but by sound. Somebody had switched on a radio or television set. It sounded like a football commentary.

Football at this hour of the morning? In spite of himself Peroni started trying to tune in to what was being said. He began to catch isolated phrases which made the subject matter of the commentary yet more baffling.

'Vast crowds . . . traditional . . . colourful and profoundly characteristic . . . feeling of tension . . .'

Sport? No, it hardly fitted with a sporting event. The commentator's voice was too hushed for one thing. World championship chess? The voice was right, but you could hardly call a chess match colourful, unless you were talking about the human one at Marostica and that wasn't this time of year.

'Over the centuries . . . very few occasions . . . disaster . . . since eighteen . . .'

An appalling idea leapt like a flying fish in Peroni's mind. Impossible. He looked at the date on his watch. Not impossible.

122

'Imploring and beseeching . . . however incomprehensible . . . very real and personal significance . . . bishop of Naples . . . outstretched . . .'

So that was the appalling truth. Three times a year, in May and December and on the nineteenth of September, the powdered blood of St Janarius liquefied, or to be more exact should and almost invariably did liquefy. Just occasionally, as the commentator had been explaining, it failed to do so, and these occasions were an infallible sign of disaster and tragedy.

Today was the twentieth of September and the blood of St Janarius had refused to liquefy. As a Neapolitan Peroni's own blood iced at the implications.

'Yesterday morning . . . eight hours of uninterrupted prayer . . .'

The voice of the commentator came to a temporary halt and the volume was turned up on the voice of Naples itself. The voice of Naples praying for the renewal of its miracle. A miracle generally held to be pointless in the more rationally calculating north, but cherished by the Neapolitans with passionate patriotism.

Peroni would have found it impossible to justify the miracle to a non-Neapolitan, to explain why the liquefaction of some dry blood, shed more than sixteen centuries before, should be so vitally important for Neapolitans everywhere today. But it was so. And the ceremony now with its fervent and unanswered prayer threw a blindingly painful light on Peroni's new and alien situation.

He had to escape.

He abandoned his office, went rapidly down the stairs and out, unhindered and unobserved, onto the Fondamenta San Lorenzo. The sound of Naples at prayer was even louder here, and he almost ran along the canal-side until it was out of earshot.

Sixteen

Vicenza is a small, but intensely individual provincial city, famous for its recipe for cooking cod, its mushrooms and the architectural stamp imposed upon it by Andrea Palladio who designed all its most famous buildings, the magnificent central square and the theatre with its scenery in dramatic *trompe l'oeil* perspective. It is embroidered by five intricate little rivers spanned by agreeably idiosyncratic bridges.

Roberti had been unable to enjoy any of these things. He was seated in a strictly functional, non-Palladian office to which an impassive MP had brought two men identified as having attended the heroin party at Jesolo.

But Roberti had succeeded in getting nothing of interest out of either of them. If he did no better with the third and so far only remaining witness he would have to go back to Jesolo empty-handed.

He looked at Mrs Randerheim who was interpreting for him. Mrs Randerheim blinked benignly at him through her pink-rimmed spectacles, but provided no inspiration.

Then he had an idea. What would *dott.* Peroni have done under the circumstances? *Dott.* Peroni didn't just ask questions, he lived them; he almost seemed to transform himself into different people according to the character of his interviewee.

But I'm not *dott.* Peroni, Roberti told himself in alarm at the mere prospect. And there the idea would probably have been abandoned if it hadn't been for an unexpected factor.

The third witness was frightened.

He was a fat GI with a face that looked as if it were made of custard with raisins for eyes. The two men who had preceded him in the chair opposite Roberti had been tough. Known addicts with nothing to lose. But this one gave out fear like a smell.

Almost spontaneously Roberti found himself being *dott.* Peroni. He looked as if he knew the secrets of the fat man's heart; his tone of voice implied that he had at his disposal unspeakable means of extracting information; his questions, even through Mrs Randerheim, were as sudden and unexpected as arrows.

Mrs Randerheim was startled at first by this transformation, then became animated like a drooping tropical plant in the rain.

And it worked. At a certain point Mrs Randerheim turned to deliver an answer to Roberti with the air of someone who has come across an undiscovered masterpiece by Giotto.

'He says he believes that maybe the big man with the girl came from the U.S. base at Naples,' she said.

The shop window was filled with television sets. There must have been twenty of them, and they ranged from a giant luxury model to a baby portable with a screen scarcely bigger than a cigarette pack. And they were all showing in perfect colour the ceremony in the cathedral at Naples.

Peroni stood transfixed before the shop window, apparently unable to escape, his eyes flicking from screen to screen. The fact that the sound was turned off made it almost worse. You didn't need the words; you could read it all too clearly on the faces. The bishop of Naples, dignified, in control of himself and the situation, but obviously under strain. The ancient crone, her still bright eyes brimming with tears. ('Great television!' you could almost hear the cameraman thinking as he closed up on her.) The very pretty girl with the cheap scarf on her head and an expression of almost child-like hope. The man with the wild squint and the ancient and tattered overcoat.

The cameras, and with them all twenty screens, cut to the riotously ornamental reliquary in which the blood was kept, and stayed there for four long seconds, the very immobility proclaiming the non-event.

Then back to the people. The nun, disappointed but still hopeful; St Janarius knows what he's at. The deacons, business-like, but showing signs of flagging. The party of schoolchildren, all with their eyes fixed on the miracle-that-wasn't except for one little boy who had spotted the television camera.

Outside the shop window, watching all those lips in colour moving in complete silence, Peroni felt his own isolation more acutely. For the first time in his life he was definitely outside St Janarius's sprawling and untidy flock.

And to make matters worse an appalling possibility had broken and entered his mind. He tried to ignore it, but the possibility was yelling itself at him.

This is all deliberate, it screamed. St Janarius is out to get you. You're being hunted.

Impossible. The blood had failed to liquefy *yesterday* before he had attended the Satanist rite. Besides, the whole vast network of circumstance as a result of which Peroni was being confronted with radio and television coverage of the ceremony in Naples couldn't have all been created just to hunt down one erring sheep.

Why not?

Peroni ripped himself away from the shop window and ran again.

A torpor settles upon Jesolo when the shops close at one o'clock and lasts till they re-open again at half-past three or four, and the streets resemble those of a western town at high noon. Benito Mussolini had the rhythm of the Jesolo day in his bones and he could tell at exactly what point it was without looking at his watch. So now he could feel that the one o'clock torpor had arrived.

He went into the back room where Desdemona was playing with some building blocks.

'Put them away nicely, *angelo mio*,' he said, 'Time we were off for lunch.'

But at that moment he heard the ting of the shop door opening.

'One more customer,' he said. 'Then we'll be off.'

He turned back into the shop and then became motionless as instantaneously as Lot's wife.

It was the quarry.

Benito had made the appointment at a bar in Via Verdi that

evening. Now it seemed that the quarry, putting together the phone call with the face he had recognised earlier that morning, had anticipated the meeting.

For the first time Benito Mussolini had an uneasy feeling he might have overplayed his hand.

The whole of Venice seemed to be following the non-liquefaction of the blood of St Janarius. Everywhere he went Peroni was pursued by the sound of radios and television sets. And it was always the same thing: the commentator's voice dinning in the failure of the blood to liquefy and the gravity of this, alternating with the massed prayer of Naples.

It was unbearable and yet appeared to be inescapable.

Suddenly Peroni emerged from a *calle* onto a water-front. Before him the large expanse of the lagoon heaved and tossed in the Bora which gave no signs of slackening.

He was on the Fondamenta Nuove. Somewhere over to his left St Janarius was continuing his pursuit, but now at last there was a way of escape.

Onto the lagoon. The worst that could follow him out into the midst of all that water was a transistor which could always be avoided.

And there, conveniently, a water-bus was waiting. He ran onto the mooring platform, fumbling in his pocket for a ticket, and then onto the boat which was almost entirely empty. He went into the forward part and sat down.

It was blessedly quiet. Now he would only have to stay on the lagoon for an hour or so and the transmission would be finished. It was ridiculous they were doing it at all, come to that, he thought. What was the use of having the RAI dominated by communists if they couldn't stop programmes like that going out?

He watched anxiously as an employee of the *Azienda Municipale Trasporti Venezia* cast off, fearful lest somebody should bring a portable television set onto the boat at the last minute. But the casting off was accomplished without incident and soon the water bus was churning and throbbing its way onto the lagoon.

He was safe.

There were four other people in the forward part of the boat, all seated with their backs to Peroni. There was a middle-aged couple, the man emersed in '*L'Unità*' while his wife kept up a ceaseless flow of what seemed to be completely silent conversation; and there were two women, one white-haired, miniscule and dressed in black, the other younger with fair hair and a green dress.

It seemed to Peroni that he had seen the younger one somewhere before, but from the back he couldn't identify her. He had a knack of staring at women's backs in such a way that they felt compelled to look round. He employed this knack now and had the satisfaction of seeing her shoulders move as though she felt his eyes upon her. She resisted the urge to look round for a couple of seconds, then, as though she were trying to do something with her hair, half turned her head so that he was able to see her face.

It was Ornella.

'Commissario!'

'Signorina!'

She seemed slightly flustered as though he had caught her in curlers, but there was the same warmth he had felt on their first encounter and she seemed pleased to see him.

He could hardly remain sitting five seats behind her so he stood up and walked with some difficulty forward on the bucking boat and shook hands with her.

'Can I introduce my mother?' she said, 'Mamma this is the famous Commissario Achille Peroni. Commissario—*la mamma*.'

He shook the old lady's tiny hand and she gave him a smile of great sweetness. '*Piacere*,' she said.

'*Piacere*,' said Peroni.

That done the three of them sat there looking amiably at each other and holding onto the back of the seats in front.

'What brings you on this trip?' Ornella asked.

'What trip is that?'

'You don't know?' Ornella looked surprised. 'We're going to the cemetery. Of course.'

128

Seventeen

Signora Vittoria knew her own stretch of Jesolo as intimately as a policeman his beat. She had been going there every year since the birth of her children who were now parents themselves. She was deeply versed in the swarming life of the beach, knowing exactly whose eldest daughter was going out with undesirable waiters, whose son had been failed at school, whose husband was drinking too much. She knew all the shopkeepers, their habits, prices and the quality of their goods.

And as she sat with her husband at lunch she was aware that something was not quite as it should be in the street below. What it was she couldn't put her finger on. Nothing exactly wrong. Nothing so definite as that. Just slightly out of place.

'What's the matter, Vittoria?'

'Nothing,' she said, 'nothing.'

'Let's be having the fish then.'

She went absently into the little curtained off kitchen, got the fish from the oven, carried it to the table and served her husband.

'Aren't you having any?'

'In a minute.'

'It'll get cold.'

She looked at the street below as she would look at one of those complicated drawings in the *Settimana Enigmistica* where you have to find out eight things which are wrong. Only here it wasn't eight, but one, if she could only spot it.

'The photographer's,' she said, spotting it, 'it's not closed.'

'So?' said her husband with a mouthful of fish.

'It's always closed at this hour.'

The opening and closing of shops were as predictable as the orbits within the solar system, and the fact that the door of the

photographer's shop did not have the blind down or the closed
sign up was as unusual as if Mercury had gone into reverse.

'Let's go and see what's happened.'

'And let the fish get cold?'

'I'll go by myself then.'

He shrugged and took another mouthful of fried fish.

When she was downstairs and across the street, Signora
Vittoria realised that something, and not just a mere *Settimana
Enigmistica* detail, really was wrong, for looking through the
shop window she could see that the place was in wild disorder as
though a herd of elephants had crashed through it.

She was nervous of going in, but curiosity had the upper hand
and she cautiously pushed open the shop door and put her head
in.

'*Permesso?*' she said. '*Permesso?*'

No answer. The place seemed deserted. And then, from
inside the little door behind the counter, she heard a whimpering sound. At first she thought it was a baby, but then she
remembered that monkey the photographer so unhygienically
pushed into children's arms.

'*Permesso?*' she repeated and went behind the counter.
'*Permesso?*'

She peeped through the little door and gasped at a spectacle
which reduced the normal beach dramas to sand-grain
proportions.

For the monkey was jumping and lamenting about the body
of its most emphatically dead master.

'You didn't realise we were going to the cemetery,
Commissario?'

Peroni realised how ridiculous the situation must seem to her.
'I happened to be on the Fondementa Nuove,' he said. 'I
thought it would help me to concentrate if I could get out on the
water for a while, and the boat was there so I just got on it.'

'I see,' she said, accepting it completely.

Peroni now saw that they were in fact heading for the walled
island of San Michele where the Venetians awaited the last
judgement. With the low white dome of its chapel and the zig-

130

zag skyward jutting of its innumerable cypresses, it lay only a few minutes chug ahead of them.

'If you want to think, Commissario,' said Ornella, 'we mustn't disturb you.'

'No, no,' said Peroni, 'I'm delighted to have your company. *Your* trip is deliberate I imagine?'

'That's right,' said Ornella. 'I take *la mamma* out there whenever I can. She likes to sit and chat with Papa.'

'Papa is—?'

'Yes.'

'I see.' He nodded with sympathetic understanding at *la mamma* and she smiled her same sweet smile at him. It was as though two people of different languages were trying to show their mutual good will.

'Any news of Kehzia?' Ornella asked.

Peroni felt an inner jolt. 'No,' he said, 'no news.'

'Oh, I'm sorry,' said Ornella, overcome with contrition, 'I shouldn't have asked.'

'No, no,' said Peroni, 'of course you can ask. It's just that there is—no news.'

'I see.' She paused a second. 'I'm sure there will be soon.'

No, there will never be any more news about Kehzia. 'What makes you so sure?' he asked.

'Well,' she said sounding flustered, 'I mean you always do get at the truth in the end, don't you? You're famous for it.'

The truth. That was something else he had abjured. 'Not always,' he said. 'The truth can be hard to come by in Italy.'

'Yes, but you—'

'Hold on—I think it's going to be a bumpy mooring in this wind.'

'Yes, you're right. Hold on tight, Mamma.'

But in spite of the Bora and the lurching of the lagoon, the *Azienda Municipale* man made a casually efficient tie-up at the tossing platform.

'I suppose you're going straight back,' said Ornella helping her mother up.

'No,' said Peroni. 'Now that I'm here I'll stay for a while.' Cemeteries were safe from television sets.

131

'That's fine,' said Ornella. 'I'll show you round if you like when *la mamma's* comfortably settled.'

Together with a handful of other passengers they went from the boat to the platform and onto the jetty with the Bora buffeting, slapping and tugging at them. Then as they passed through a doorway they found themselves in sudden sanctuary. They were in a large cloister, and they could hear the Bora howling outside as though in frustration at having let them slip through its fingers.

Having crossed the cloister they entered the cemetery proper. As they went in Peroni looked at the various admonishments to visitors and couldn't help reading the notice in English. *You are in a cemetery*, it said. *You are not allowed to behave indecently.*

'Papa's over there,' said Ornella, 'among the military.'

'He was a soldier?' asked Peroni.

'No,' she said, 'a *carabiniere*, but it counts as the same thing.'

Cheea might have been a mishearing or a diminutive of Kehzia, but if you spelt it Cia, it was also a diminutive of Lucia. Taking this as a starting point, Perez had collected all the missing persons reports concerning people called Lucia. It was surprising how many there were.

He was now carefully going through these.

Lucia Arbizzoli. The photograph hardly fitted the American's description of the female as "pretty lush", but Perez, who was cautious, didn't yet eliminate her.

Lucia Fasol. She looked the part more, but all the circumstances pointed to her having been drowned six months previously.

Lucia Piccoli. Appearance, age and height were right. She was unmarried and a teacher. At the time of her disappearance just over a month previously she had been living with her parents in Padua. She had left her home one morning in August and simply not returned. The parents could think of no motives for her voluntarily going off, but admitted she had been acting strangely lately (drugs?) and suspected she might have been having trouble in her private life of which they knew nothing.

Not a lot, but on all points this Lucia *could* have been the girl at the heroin party. It was worth a visit to Padua.

At this point the Jesolo police chief, Zilli, came in. 'Somebody's just reported finding a body,' he said, 'apparently that of the photographer called Benito Mussolini.'

A cemetery wasn't the ideal place for being alone with a man like Achille Peroni, but beggars can't be choosers and any place was better than none. She just hoped she wouldn't muck the opportunity up. He certainly didn't seem to *mind* being with her; come to that he even seemed quite pleased. But he was also looking strained, as if he had something on his mind. It would be nice if she could cheer him up a bit, make him relax, but with her sure-fire capacity for always saying the wrong thing to the right man she would have to be very careful how she went about it. A bit of light chat was what was needed.

Ornella and Peroni were walking together in silence having just left *la mamma*. The old lady had immediately set to changing the flowers and at the same time quite unselfconsciously telling her late husband all the news of herself, Ornella and their family and friends.

'The ecclesiastics are all over there,' said Ornella, hoping that might pass for light chat. 'Personally, poor dears, I'd have thought they'd much rather be mixed up with all the other people. I mean they're isolated enough when they're alive so they'd probably like a bit of a change when they're dead.'

'You'd think so.'

But his heart wasn't in it. She cast about for some other topic, but he anticipated her.

'Your father must have been young when he died,' he said, 'to judge by the photograph on the tomb.'

She felt the lurch she always felt at mention of her father's death. Should she tell him? Why not? 'He was killed.'

'Killed? How?'

'Oh, it's an old story now. I was tiny when it happened. He was coming home one night late, going off duty, when he saw two men, one of whom he recognised as being wanted. He stopped them for questioning, but one of them pulled a gun and shot him.'

133

They passed a long avenue of flower-decked wall tombs like a necro-supermarket.

'At least that was how we thought it happened,' went on Ornella, 'but a couple of months later one of the two men was arrested—not the one who shot Papa. He described what really happened. When Papa stopped them, the other man pulled a gun, but he didn't shoot immediately. He held Papa covered and offered him a million lire to let them go. In those days a million lire was an enormous sum, and the *Carabinieri* were even worse paid than they are now. And the men had the money with them. They'd done a bank job that day, and they were ready to hand it over just like that. Papa could have walked home with a million lire and nobody need ever have known. He and *la mamma* could have had everything they wanted. But he said no. Three times the man offered him the money and three times he refused it. So he was shot.'

Children, like ecclesiastics and the military, are grouped together on San Michele and they passed these little tombs in silence. Some were attended by angels, all had the photographs of their infant ocupants. Ornella found herself instinctively looking at the dates to see how long they had lived. Seven years. Three years. Less than a day. Two weeks. She also observed Peroni covertly. He seemed more disturbed than she would have expected at the story of her father's death.

'I don't usually tell people about it nowadays,' she said when they had passed the avenue of children, 'it so often embarrasses them. But you're a policeman like he was, so it's different. But I do get angry—inside anyway—when people go on about everything and everybody in Italy being corrupt, as though it were a generally accepted fact. Then I think about Papa who chose death rather than taking a bribe. And I think of all the other honest and incorruptible people. Because they're the people who are keeping Italy alive. And you can find them everywhere. In schools, in the hospitals, in shops, in the country. In the police. The people like you, Commissario.'

Peroni was silent for so long that she stole another look at him and was shattered at the expression on his face. It was not, however, an expression she could recognise. Sorrow? Anguish?

Rage?

But whatever it was, it began to seem horribly to Ornella that once again she had said the wrong thing to the right man.

The lunch-time torpor of Jesolo was broken by the frenetic activity in and about the shop of the late Benito Mussolini. There were three police cars outside it, one with its blue roof-light still flashing round and round, while a growing crowd was milling about on the pavement trying to peer through the window.

In the small room behind the counter, Benito Mussolini, after so many years of photographing other people, was being photographed himself. He wouldn't have found the result flattering, but then he wouldn't be seeing it. One policeman was preparing to chalk an outline of the body and another was eyeing Desdemona as though he would have liked to ask her to dance, but couldn't pluck up the courage.

In the shop itself Perez was questioning Signora Vittoria whose emotional state was flickering between horror at her discovery and triumph at being in the very centre of the biggest drama Jesolo had ever seen.

'But you saw nobody entering the shop before that?' asked Perez.

'No—o,' she had to admit reluctantly. 'You see we'd only just sat down to lunch and before that I'd been in the kitchen.'

'Your husband?'

She sniffed. 'He never lifts his nose out of his paper.'

'And when you came down, did you notice anybody about in the street?'

She started as she realised the import of the question. 'You mean—?'

'I mean *anybody*, Signora.'

'I didn't actually see anybody,' she was obliged to admit. But the fact that she might have been alone in the street with the Jesolo strangler sent the value of her story rocketing even higher.

When he had finished with her, Perez went into the back room and looked at the chaos the killer had left behind him.

135

'The only thing we can be sure of for the movement,' he said, 'is that he was looking for something and, the shop being what it is, it seems likely that that something was a photograph.'

'Yes,' said the Jesolo police chief, Zilli, 'and there's something else. Just over two weeks ago, this shop was broken into at night and a similar search was made.'

'Interesting,' said the albino detective. 'Do we know anything more about that?'

'Enquiries are still being made.'

'So somebody must have been looking for a photograph—or a negative—which they didn't find. And they tried again today. But why wait for two weeks? And why strangle the photographer on the second occasion?'

'It must have been a *very* incriminating photograph,' said Zilli, 'if somebody was prepared to murder for it.'

'Very,' agreed Perez. 'And did whoever-it-was get hold of it this time?'

There was a sudden scuffle in the doorway between the shop and the back room and Desdemona swung out and onto the counter where she sat looking defiantly about her. The two men looked at her.

'If only that monkey could talk,' said Perez.

Just how they had got there Peroni would have been unable to say, but they were now in that part of the cemetery which is dedicated to the Greek and Russian Orthodox and to those who are described mysteriously as Acatholics.

Ici repose . . .
Hier ruhet in Gott . . .
Here lies . . .

Peroni could have wished that he were one of those who lay here. St Janarius had hounded him across Venice and then, just when he thought he had escaped at last, had caught him in the deadliest snare of all.

The television sets he had been able to outface, but this girl with the wry sense of humour directed always at herself, with the sweet old mother and the dead *Carabiniere* father—she was an altogether different matter.

136

In choosing her, St Janarius had shown himself to be a consummate master of his art. If she had known she was doing his work for him she would have been easier to resist, but she was altogether unaware of what she was doing, and that made her almost irresistible.

Almost? Or completely? The new self was making a last ditch stand.

'Ezra Pound,' she said. 'I'm always meaning to find out who he was, but I never get round to it. He must have been famous though, because they've put up an arrow pointing to his tomb. Oh, look—somebody's put a rose on it. A single red rose. Isn't that romantic?'

The words she said no longer mattered. Her voice worked in him by itself, even when the subject matter was Ezra Pound and a single red rose.

'*Princesse Catherine Bagration decedéà Venise le 11 Juin 1857.* I did French at school. Hardly Comédie Française level, but it's just about up to an epitaph . . .'

He suddenly realised that she was miserable, too, and that made it even worse. For some mysterious reason he had made her miserable, and all this bright, graveyard talk was just a cover-up.

'*Princesse C. Troubetzkoy nèe Moussin Pouchkin.* It's a very aristocratic part of the world we're in, isn't it?'

If the image of himself in the blackbird's eye had been a true one, he wouldn't have cared whether she was miserable or not, he realised with a shock.

'Igor Stravinsky. As a matter of fact, I *do* know who he was. I remember when he died. A lovely funeral it was with a whole fleet of gondolas . . .'

Those were the words, but through them Peroni heard others. "I think about Papa who chose death rather than taking a bribe. And I think of all the other honest and incorruptible people. Because they're the people who are keeping Italy alive. And you can find them everywhere . . ."

'*Aspasia widow of H. M. Alexander King of the Hellenes* . . .'

"In the schools, in the hospitals, in shops, in the country. In the police. The people like you, Commissario."

Suddenly it was over. And if all the kingdoms of the world and the glory of them had been on immediate offer, the issue could not have been reversed. For the image in the blackbird's eye no longer existed. Or rather it had never really existed; it had been a monstrous illusion with as much substance as a nightmare and, like a nightmare on waking, it had vanished.

One day he would tell Ornella what had really happened on the cemetery island of San Michele.

'I must go back to Jesolo, Signorina,' he said. 'I've got a lot to do.'

She looked horribly stricken as though her worst fears had been confirmed. 'But—didn't you say you wanted to concentrate?' she stuttered awkwardly.

'I have concentrated,' he said, 'and I've come up with the answer I was looking for. Thanks to you.' He held out his hand.

She looked doubtful. Then slowly pleasure tinged the edges of the doubt and she took the offered hand.

'I'll tell you about it some day,' said Peroni.

It was scarcely even a surprise to Peroni when, some time later that day, he learned that the blood of St Janarius had at last liquefied, and that the liquefaction had taken place at almost exactly the moment when he and Ornella had been standing in front of the tomb of Aspasia widow of HM Alexander King of the Hellenes.

Old Rita

Eighteen

Everything about *Prof.* Piccoli was boring: his voice, his appearance, his teaching. He emanated boredom like a poisonous gas which withered all about him—the literature he taught, his relationships with pupils and colleagues and, worst of all, his family life. For, though he could do nothing about it, he was in no doubt that it was thanks to him Elena was a faded, indifferent automat while their daughter, Lucia, had become— what she had become.

Prof. Piccoli finished school at eleven o'clock that morning. As always he closed his register, coughed, settled his spectacles on his nose, collected books and register, rose and left the classroom in exactly that order. Having left books and register in the staff room, he went down the stairs and out of the school, saying '*Buon giorno*' to the porter with the identical inflection he had used some ten thousand times during his career at the school. It bored the porter; it bored him; there was no escape from it.

During the brief walk from school to home, both in the outskirts of Padua, he thought about his daughter whom he had bored to her ruin. Just what form that ruin had taken he didn't know, but there could be no doubt it was ruin.

Could it have been avoided? He had asked himself this question many times since her disappearance just over a month before and now, as on all the previous occasions, he got no answer.

Having reached the block of flats where they lived, he collected the post (even that was boring: two soap advertisements and the telephone bill) and took the lift up to the second floor. When he had unlocked the door and was hanging his hat on the peg, Elena came out of the living room.

'Enrico,' she said, 'there's a policeman come to see us about Lucia.'

A needle of fear pierced the wadding of dullness which insulated him from the current of life.

Perez registered a zero albino count. Neither the bleached and lifeless woman nor her schoolteacher husband who had just entered had even noticed his appearance. They probably wouldn't have noticed if he'd been an African witch doctor in full regalia.

'Is there news of Lucia?' The voice was of a deadly monotony, but behind it Perez could sense fear.

'We have found a trace of a girl who might be Lucia,' he said carefully. 'You may be able to help us decide.' They sat in armchairs enveloped in plastic wrappers. 'The report on her disappearance,' he went on, 'indicated that she had been acting strangely before she went away and you thought that could have been consonant with drugs. Can you tell me more about that?'

'It's so difficult for us,' said the woman. 'We don't know anything about that sort of thing, you see. Drugs . . .' She gestured feebly.

'You implied that her private life was not very satisfactory,' Perez tried a new tack. 'In what way?'

They looked at each other hopelessly. 'She didn't tell us about it,' said the schoolteacher. 'She didn't tell us about anything.' It sounded like a plea for help.

'The girl whose traces we have found,' proceeded Perez, changing direction again, 'was in Jesolo. Can you think of any reason why your daughter might go to Jesolo?'

They looked at each other again. 'We used to go there every year,' said the woman, 'when she was a little girl. Then it began to get vulgar so we changed to Eraclea.'

Something, thought Perez. Not much, but something. In the scales which were weighing Kehzia and Lucia as the dead girl at the heroin party a small handful of sand had dropped into Lucia's scale.

'She was a teacher,' he said. 'She took after you?'

142

The schoolmaster smiled a wintry non-smile. 'Our attitudes to the profession were scarcely comparable.'

'What subject did she teach?'

'English.'

Perez stiffened. The girl at the party had spoken English. Then he relaxed, remembering his own English studies at school: not a single one of the teachers he had come across had ever spoken anything remotely approaching fluent English.

'But did she,' he tried just to make sure, 'did she actually speak English?'

'Well, no,' said her father. 'Before she started teaching she worked with the Americans. She spoke fluent American.'

A large bucketful of sand fell into Lucia's scale.

Getting back to reality was not so much heroic as laborious. He had been away from it for less than twenty-four hours and yet the return made him feel like Rip Van Winkle. The main reason for this was that his mind and soul had covered such immeasurable distances while his body had been in the de Sanctis palace and on the island cemetery of San Michele.

A good subsidiary reason was that the murder of Benito Mussolini had occurred during his absence.

The first thing that Peroni asked himself was whether there could be any connection between that murder and the disappearance of Kehzia. And could such a connection have anything to do with the problem that puzzled him almost more than any other: why had de Sanctis so badly wanted him out of Jesolo? Ostensibly, the only reason for thinking there might be a connection between the murder and the disappearance was that Jesolo was not the sort of place in which such things normally happened so that when two of them *did* happen within a short time of each other it was natural to think they were linked.

Somewhere in the overcrowded Neapolitan street market which was Peroni's mind, he suspected that there was another reason, too, but poke about in the confusion though he might, he couldn't trace it. If he pretended to ignore it, maybe it would jump out at him.

In the meantime there was a conference about the Mussolini murder.

The table at which they were seated was strewn with photographs and negatives. Children and adults of half a dozen nationalities were clutching Desdemona who looked with an air of complicity at the camera lens. There were chunky-looking Americans with taurine necks and close-cropped hair, long legged and long haired little girls, elderly couples, Germans with large stomachs, English package tourists whose expressions indicated a profound distrust of foreign photographers and their monkeys. All these had to be gone through, but as they were almost certainly the killer's rejects the task was a thankless one.

'Is it possible,' said *dott*. Amabile, head of the venetian police, with scholastic disapproval, 'that *nobody* was seen going into the shop? It was broad daylight in the centre of Jesolo!'

'But at one o'clock,' Zilli, the Jesolo police chief, reminded him, 'The whole place is switched off completely at that hour.'

'And the flats opposite?'

'We've been through them all. A lot of them are empty by now and the occupants of the rest, like Signora Vittoria, were either in their kitchens or at table.'

Dott. Amabile clicked with irritation; he disliked murder, considering it irrational and untidy, and he abhorred it when it attracted unusual publicity, as this one was doing because of the victim's name.

'This other business,' he said, 'the disappearance of the American girl—is there any possibility of a connection?'

There were glances about the table; most people had envisaged the possibility of a connection, but nobody had been able to go further than that.

Suddenly there was a gunshot crack which had reflexes leaping until it was realised that the sound came from Peroni who had been fingering a biro throughout the conference and had now snapped it in two.

'The two weeks' gap!' he said, having suddenly spotted the reason amid the colourful chaos of the Neapolitan street market.

The others looked at him with the polite tolerance of northerners regarding an over exuberant southerner.

'The two week's gap,' Peroni repeated. 'That's the connection. Somebody broke into Benito Mussolini's shop two weeks ago in search of an incriminating photograph or negative which they didn't find. Two weeks later the same person went back, killed Mussolini and made another search. But why after two weeks?'

Peroni seemed to realise that the rhetorical question was a bit much, for at this stage he switched his disquisition into a less dramatic key.

'It was the *Gazzettino*,' he said. 'The *Gazzettino* came out the day before yesterday with the photograph of Kehzia Michaelis. Mussolini must have recognised her as somebody he had photographed *with somebody else*. And he guessed that the person who had broken into his shop two weeks before had been after the photograph because it established a link between him and Kehzia. He then got in touch with the person and tried to blackmail him. Which resulted in his murder. In other words,' he concluded, now almost overdoing northern reserve, 'Mussolini was killed because he recognised somebody involved in the disappearance of Kehzia Michaelis. That's the connection.'

This was met with the silence of northerners facing a wild, but apparently incontrovertible southern tale.

And in the silence the telephone suddenly shrilled.

Zilli picked it up. 'For you, *dottore*,' he said to Roberti after listening a second.

'*Pronto*?' said Roberti, '*Si*.' He pulled a notepad towards him and started to write. '*Si*,' he said, '*Si* . . .'

'That was Naples,' he said when he had finished. 'The American Military Police have got the man who looks like a boxer, the one at the heroin party. It seems he's a drug runner, and that's what he was doing up here—he'd brought a consignment of drugs to sell at the Vicenza base. He admits he was at the party in Jesolo.'

Roberti turned towards Peroni. 'He denies that the girl was

dead,' he said , 'He says she'd just passed out. She recovered during the drive and he dropped her off in Florence. They asked him about the name, too. He said he didn't know the surname, but she told him her name was Cia, short for Lucia. Not Kehzia.

So the girl at the drug party wasn't Kehzia at all. There wasn't any evidence to suggest that Kehzia had even been on drugs. Roberti's announcement had lopped off an entire branch from the trunk of enquiries at one go, sending Peroni spinning on to the next branch which was that of the Mussolini killing.

Was it possible, he thought, for somebody to be killed in the main street of Jesolo in the middle of the day without anybody seeing anything?

Then out of the blue with disconcerting swiftness, there came one of Peroni's more outrageous ideas.

Peroni's hand was raised to open the door. Then he let it fall again, submerged by a wave of diffidence and embarrassment. Instead, he went into the bar next door and ordered himself a *grappa*.

The idea was altogether impossible. True, unlike most of Peroni's wilder schemes, it didn't involve danger. But it did involve looking ridiculous which was almost worse. He would gladly have abandoned the whole thing if the old man's advice hadn't continued to echo in his head like a tune you can't get rid of.

And just suppose there were some truth in it. Just suppose it worked. What a Peroni *coup* it would make—what a story!

The idea had come to him on a wave of exhilaration resulting from Roberti's Neapolitan news, immediately followed by Perez's story about Lucia Piccoli in Padua. It was now virtually certain that Kehzia had not died at the Jesolo heroin party. Which meant that the hunt for her would have to start all over again. Immediately ideas started to tumble in his mind. Ideas concerning de Sanctis, Don Zaccaria, Luca Zambelli . . . This idea.

He swallowed the *grappa* in one, shuddered, and let the impetus of it propel him next door, devoutly hoping nobody would be there.

146

But the door opened and there, at a desk, was a supercilious looking young man in a white coat, just the sort Peroni was most dreading.

'*Si*?' said the young man.

'*Questura*,' said Peroni, acquiring a momentary advantage which he knew he was going to throw away with interest. 'I understand you're keeping a monkey here for us.'

'That's right. Er—Desdemona.'

'I'd like to see her.'

'By all means. She's in a bad way, though. Pining—won't eat anything. I don't expect her to survive much longer.'

Peroni already knew this.

They went through the outer surgery into a ward where half a dozen variously stricken animals were lying. The only monkey, evidently Desdemona, was huddled motionless in the corner of a large cage.

'See what I mean?' said the vet, 'She's very low indeed. And the trouble being psychological rather than physical there's precious little I can do about it. Monkeys are sensitive animals.'

'Can we have her out of the cage?'

The vet shrugged, then opened the cage and lifted Desdemona out, putting her on the floor where she took up the same inert position.

'Does she—er bite?' asked Peroni. He was never particularly at ease with animals, a fact which made his present undertaking even more absurd.

'No,' said the vet, 'she's exceptionally tame.'

With all his heart Peroni wished he would leave them alone together so that he could make a fool of himself in private, but he showed no sign of moving.

'Desdemona,' tried Peroni, kneeling warily beside her. '*Ciao*, Desdemona.'

The monkey looked up at him for a moment with lack-lustre eyes, then down at the floor again.

'How about a bit of cheese? Parmesan—nothing but the best.'

He got from his pocket the chunk which he had bought on the way there, unwrapped it, broke off a piece and offered it to

147

the monkey. In her state, it was ridiculous to expect she would take it, let alone eat it. And indeed she merely eyed the cheese suspiciously.

'Desdemona,' said Peroni, feeling more of a fool than ever, 'just to please me.'

Again he heard the voice of the old man in Naples who had lived in a single room with half a dozen monkeys and conversed with them as though they were intelligent children. 'An ailing monkey,' he had said, 'will always be tempted by Parmesan cheese.' Well, maybe the old man could always tempt them with Parmesan cheese, but that didn't mean that other people could.

'Desdemona,' pleaded Peroni. 'Nice cheese.'

It was no good. He would have to abandon the lunatic venture and retreat before the scathing, mute contempt of the young vet.

And then with all the sensational unexpectedness of the heavens splitting open, Desdemona stretched out her right paw and took the cheese. She turned it over several times, sniffed it and started to gnaw it. The rhythm of her chewing accelerated as she went. She finished the piece and then looked up at Peroni expectantly. He broke off another piece and gave it to her, looking up as he did so at the vet whose expression had changed to one of awed amazement.

But Peroni knew his triumph was to be short lived, for the old man's second piece of advice would plunge him yet more deeply into a sea of contempt from which there would be no rescue.

'If ever you want to know something from a monkey,' he had said, 'just ask. Ask and go on asking. Sooner or later they'll understand what you want and they'll find a way of telling you. Just ask.'

Peroni postponed the moment of humiliation by giving Desdemona another bit of Parmesan. The fact that she was eating it at all was an achievement, but the journey from that to a full-scale police interrogation was like getting from the moon to another galaxy.

'Desdemona,' said Peroni when he had decided it could be put off no longer, 'you saw it happen. Who killed him, Desdemona? Who came into the shop yesterday at lunchtime?'

148

He could feel the vet's appalled disbelief boring into his neck like a gimlet, but there was no going back now; he had staked his apparent sanity on the old man's advice and he would have to go through with the bet.

'Who was it, Desdemona? You *know*, don't you? You saw him! Tell me who it was!'

It was just a question of time, Peroni realised, before the vet sent for those other white coated men.

'Tell me, Desdemona! It's the only thing you can do for him now. Find a way of telling me!'

The absurd thing was that he seemed to be falling into the way of it; it was no longer artificial and strained, but almost spontaneous. And the reason it was spontaneous, he realised with sudden incredulity, was that he was communicating with the monkey. It was as though she were used to human speech. She might not be following it all, but something was getting through to her. Peroni felt a kick of power.

'I know you can find some way of telling me, Desdemona. Think! Try and tell me! Who was it, Desdemona?'

And the monkey was transformed. She was no longer the listless, half dead creature he had seen lying in the cage; it was as though she had been re-charged with life. She was jumping up and down beside Peroni, chattering at him.

'Slowly,' he said, slackening the rhythm of his own speech, 'Who killed him, Desdemona? Who was it?'

The monkey's excitement became somewhat attenuated in response to Peroni's *rallentando*, but her gibbering was predictably as incomprehensible as ever.

Peroni tried several times more, but although the monkey continued to respond enthusiastically, there was not the smallest grain of sense in her replies. Obviously the old man had meant, not that monkeys could communicate with mankind at large, but that he himself had come to understand their talk.

Peroni got up. 'It was a stupid idea,' he said.

'As far as your investigation is concerned it's produced no results,' said the vet, 'but from a medical point of view it's almost miraculous.'

'Well, that's something, I suppose,' said Peroni.

149

He was about to go when a thought occurred to him. 'As a vet,' he said, 'would you consider it possible to find a blackbird—or at any rate a bird that is black—as big as that.' He indicated with his hand the size of the bird at the Satanist rite.

'As big as that, no,' said the vet, 'Quite impossible. But you can find some remarkably big birds. There are some in a large private aviary just outside Treviso. Owned by a man called de Sanctis.'

Nineteen

Peroni's sister, Assunta, was in a bad mood. It was partly the fault of the Bora which was keeping them all cooped up in the flat on top of one another. It was also the children who were bickering endlessly. They would drive her mad, she told herself, seriously mad. She would have to go into a clinic and then what would happen to them? She slammed into the tiny kitchen to find some escape.

And there was Achille, too. He was behaving in a most extraordinary way, banging out of the flat when they were talking about the missing girl with the ridiculous name and then going to Satanist rites. True, when he had told her the somewhat garbled tale the evening before he had said that it was all part of the investigation and that he didn't believe in it for an instant. But she took leave to doubt that. No Neapolitan ever disbelieves quite so sweepingly in anything super-natural.

She heard the doorbell ring and the children literally falling over each other to answer it.

'*Ciao*, Uncle Achille!'

Fortunately there was enough *risotto* to go round, though he really might say when he was coming to lunch.

'Anything more about the late bull-frog of the Pontine Marshes, Uncle Achille?'

'Or about Kehzia?'

'Well, in a flash of brilliance exceptional even for me I've established a link between the two. It was the two weeks' gap between the . . .'

Assunta faded out her brother's voice. The children always

151

pestered him with questions about his work and he seemed to enjoy answering, as though it were a sort of game. But because she always had too much to do, while they of course never lifted a finger, she never followed all their reasonings and felt with resentment that she was excluded from them. And this resentment, though she would never admit it, was partly due to the fact that the children said such clever things while she never managed to produce any ideas at all.

She took cutlery and plates for Achille into the living room. '*Ciao*, Achille.' They were so absorbed in their discussion that they ignored her. As usual.

'I mean there's no body,' she half heard Anna Maria saying. 'It's difficult nowadays to have a murder without a body.'

'With the sea right outside the front door?'

She faded them out and went to get the wine and mineral water, at the same time tasting the risotto on the tip of a fork. It was ready. She served it, shepherded them—still talking—to the table and filled their plates. They ate automatically; nobody dreamed of complimenting her on the cooking.

' . . . de Sanctis and Don Zaccaria,' she heard her brother saying, 'Not to mention the young man called Luca Zambelli. Those are the three we know to have been involved . . . I've started enquiries about all three, but no results so far.'

Assunta felt something stir at the back of her mind and realised it must have something to do with what they were talking about.

De Sanctis, they had said, Don Zaccaria and Luca somebody-or-other. The first and the last she discounted at once, not knowing anything about either of them.

That left Don Zaccaria. In a sense she'd known him ever since they had been coming to Jesolo, for they invariably went to his church for Mass on Sunday. But such knowledge as one might glean of a priest in church was scarcely likely to be of interest in a police investigation.

And yet there was something else. She frowned in concentration. Then she remembered.

The grocer's wife.

Jesolo had a small skeleton population which lived on there all through the year, and the grocer and his wife were part of it. She was curious and a gossip and she knew all there was to know about all the other residents of the ghost lido in winter. Not least about her parish priest, Don Zaccaria.

Assunta remembered a long talk they had had about him and, in particular, one detail which had struck her at the time as being unusual. She felt a little stirring of satisfaction at the thought that for once she would be able to outdo her children.

'Don Zaccaria, Achille,' she said, 'I do know one thing about him—he's an officially nominated exorcist.'

Monsignore Roccaforte, the rector of the seminary, was, as his surname suggested, a stronghold of a man with a craggy, stern face, iron-grey hair and a lean, muscular body. Because he was soldierly in the tradition of St Ignatius Loyola, he accepted in a spirit of discipline the reforms of Vatican II, but insofar as he was able without transgressing orders, he ruled the seminary in a pre-Conciliar spirit.

Above all he mistrusted secular interference in matters clerical which meant that he strongly disapproved of the presence of a policeman who had just arrived and was standing at the other side of his massive, altar-like desk.

There was, however, nothing to be done about it. A telephone call from the Cardinal Patriarch's secretary had made it clear that His Eminence authorised the visit and required such information as the policeman needed to be made available to him.

But that wouldn't stop *Mons.* Roccaforte from making his visitor's going as hard as might be. '*Sì?*' he said in a tone with which he would have received a seminarist caught reading *Madame Bovary*.

At this the policeman took *Mons.* Roccaforte off his guard by moving round to the side of the desk, kneeling, taking his hand and kissing the pastoral ring. This was a usage which had largely gone out in recent years and *Mons.* Roccaforte much regretted its passing. Of course the man was a southerner and such practices died harder in the south; still the action redounded to his credit. '*Si*?' said *Mons*. Roccaforte in a slightly less chilly tone.

'I hope you will forgive this visit, *Eminenza*, but I am required to make it by my superiors. And I assure you that nothing you may tell me will ever be made known to anybody unless it is expressly required in the interests of justice, and even then only with the greatest discretion.'

The little speech was fairly peppered with mollifiers: the *Eminenza* at the start, the reference to superiors, the assurance of silence, the respectful mention of justice, the promise of discretion.

'How can I help you?' Compared to the tone of the opening monosyllable, the phrase amounted to a throwing open of the seminary doors.

'We need to know something more about one of your seminarians, *Eminenza*, a certain Luca Zambelli.'

Mons. Roccaforte already knew that, having been informed by the Cardinal Patriarch's secretary, and it constituted one of the more puzzling aspects of the affair. The young man in question was, so far as he knew, altogether unimpeachable. There was, indeed, the one slight irregularity, but that could hardly be considered his fault.

'Please ask any questions you wish,' said *Mons*. Roccaforte with a slight inclination of his head.

'Luca Zambelli must be somewhere in his thirties,' said the policeman. 'That means his vocation was a somewhat late one, doesn't it?'

'Somewhat, but not exceptionally so, and certainly none the less valid.'

'He's given you no reason to doubt its validity?'

'None whatsoever.'

The policeman appeared to hesitate, then went on. 'What do you know of his life before he came to the seminary?'

'Being an orphan, the earlier part of it was spent largely in institutions. Then, after having obtained his degree and before initiating his studies for the priesthood, he worked for some

154

years as a teacher.'

'You say he's as orphan. Has he no relatives?'

'I understand there is some sort of uncle whom he visits from time to time. Otherwise I know of no relatives. But if you will forgive me interrupting you, Commissario,' *Mons.* Roccaforte went on, 'it might save us both time if you were to examine this. When you have done so I will gladly answer any further questions you may wish to put to me.' He picked up the file which he had had brought to him immediately on learning of police interest in Luca Zambelli and handed it across the desk to the policeman.

Assunta's revelation had jerked the picture into focus. Peroni, having finished his lunch, had driven straight to the presbytery where he had received the usual hostile welcome from Bo, the sacristan. Don Zaccaria was resting, he said, and had given strict instructions that he was not to be disturbed. Peroni had insisted and Bo had finally given way with grinding ill grace.

Don Zaccaria's rood screen of silence gave way before Peroni's newly acquired knowledge, and the story, of which Peroni had already begun to guess the general lines, was pieced together at last.

De Sanctis had indeed met Kehzia at the Dolce Vita and had introduced her into his Satanist circle. Her reactions there had been similar to Peroni's. Incredulous distaste had been followed by growing fascination at what was being offered her: the possibility to develop her random folk singing into realms of international stardom. She had allowed herself to be enmeshed.

But then one day she had met Luca. (Had he been put in her path by some wily colleague of St Janarius?) And this new relationship had fostered in her a disgust at the new self which was growing so robustly as a result of her consent to the Satanic alliance. Then she had told Luca of her involvement and he had taken her to Don Zaccaria.

'It was not a case of possession in the common sense,' said the priest after a meditative neigh, 'but I became increasingly

155

convinced that it *was* possession nevertheless. She didn't rave or fall into convulsions, but her soul was entirely in the possession of the diabolical powers to which she had voluntarily consigned it.'

Peroni shuddered inwardly. 'And did you free it?'

'I believe I was in the process of doing so.'

'When she disappeared?'

'Yes. You see there are exorcisms and exorcisms. The general public is only aware of the more spectacular sort where the initiative lies entirely with the exorcist who succeeds in casting out the evil spirit by a single act of power. But there are other cases where the battle may be drawn out over days or weeks, and in these cases the exorcist does not have the entire initiative. He can only ally himself with the forces of good and try to succour them.'

'Do you mean that this girl was a sort of battlefield for the forces of good and evil?'

'We are all that.'

'But to a greater extent than usual?'

'Yes.'

'Might that not explain her disappearance? Torn by the conflict between de Sanctis and the forces he had aroused in her on the one hand and you with the opposing forces on the other, might she not have just—escaped from both of you?'

'That is what I suspected when you told me of her disappearance.'

'And do you still think it's possible?'

Don Zaccaria gave another thoughtful neigh and shook his long head and neck as though to dispel the flies. 'Yes,' he said, 'I do.'

Europe is increasingly filled with young people, jobless, homeless, without documents or destinations, wandering gypsy-like from place to place. And it was now a real possibility that Kehzia was one of them. The prospect was still bleak, but less bleak than death.

'If it were so,' said Peroni after a pause, 'this conflict that you talk about, how would it be likely to be resolved without your help?'

156

'That would be in the hands of God,' said Don Zaccaria.

'And of the Devil?'

The priest raised his sad, drooping eyes to look into Peroni's, but gave no answer.

Peroni had once read of a minor old master which had been found in a cellar, begrimed and partially mildewed. After a superficial cleaning its quality was recognised, but something odd was seen in the attitudes of the figures it portrayed. Some were on their knees, some were fleeing, some were rooted with terror; but all apparently for no reason. Then the picture had been more carefully cleaned and the motive became apparent in the shape of a figure (A devil? A god? Peroni could no longer remember) which was making its appearance in one corner and had been hitherto obscured by the dirt.

The present situation was a bit like that. Something was missing which would put the whole scene in a different light. Something or somebody.

This belief had led him, following a series of telephone calls in high places, to the imposing *Mons*. Roccaforte and the file which was now being handed him across the desk. He thanked the *Monsignore* with the air of mystical Neapolitan fervour he had absent-mindedly assumed and started to look through the file.

If Luca had been applying to join the CIA it could scarcely have been more exhaustive. All too conscious of the relentless ecclesiastical stare fixed upon him, Peroni decided it would have to be gone through systematically, and he turned to the first page. As he did so two words smacked up at him from it: Jesolo village.

It corresponded to the heading Place of Birth, and although there was no reason Luca should not have been born in Jesolo village, it struck Peroni as an odd coincidence that he should have been.

But he hadn't finished reflecting on that when a second surprise was propelled at him from the page.

"Parentage," it said, "Iolanda Zambelli, spinster, dead."

157

So Luca had been born in Jesolo village of an illegitimate union. Peroni began to wonder whether a figure might not be emerging from beneath the grime of this particular seascape.

Twenty

The next move was planned and Peroni would have made it at once if, on calling in at the Jesolo police headquarters, he had not been told that two people were waiting to see him and would not speak to anybody else. The look that accompanied this information suggested there was something unusual about the couple.

As soon as he entered the room where they were waiting for him he saw what this was. One of them was a mongol. She must have been nearly thirty, but you could see that her mind had stayed behind for the best part of quarter of a century. As soon as she saw Peroni she made a noise that was something between a grunt and a pant.

'Shh, Isabella,' said the square, elderly, tough looking woman who was accompanying her. 'Be a good girl. Commissario Peroni?' she went on, turning to him.

'Yes?' said Peroni, covering up embarrassment with a slight overdose of Neapolitan charm.

'Pizzini,' said the woman introducing herself with a firm, masculine handshake. 'I see in the paper that you're in charge of the investigation into the disappearance of that American girl.'

Peroni felt a lurch that was part fear, part excitement. 'That's right,' he said.

'Well, my daughter Isabella here,' said the woman, 'saw something on the beach on Sunday night which I think you should hear. I'd have brought her before, but I've only just realised what it might mean. You see, she's been talking about it since Monday, but it took me a while to realise what she thought she'd seen. And it's only today that I've understood what she might really have seen.'

As she talked Peroni was uncomfortably conscious of the fact

159

that the mongol was ogling him as though he were a particularly rich and expensive cake in a shop window.

'Isabella,' the woman went on, 'tell the Commissario what you saw on Sunday night.'

A sly, knowing expression appeared on the mongol's face. 'Man,' she said with an enunciation Peroni could only just make out. 'Woman.' At this she held her hands out in front of her at shoulder level and started to jerk her body backwards and forwards at the same time giggling with her mouth open.

'Signora,' said Peroni after some seconds of this, 'it might be quicker if you were to tell me.'

'Very well,' said the woman, 'but I felt you should hear at least part of it from Isabella herself. She is the witness. And a very reliable one, too, once you have understood what she is trying to say, for she is only capable of telling exactly what she sees.'

A blunt woman, thought Peroni, but you probably have to be blunt to bring up a daughter like that. 'Please go on,' he said.

'We are on holiday here,' she said. 'We have a small flat on the first floor of the San Diego block. Isabella's room overlooks the beach, and she sometimes watches the couples on the beach doing their things.' She stated this flatly as a fact. 'There was a bit of a moon on Sunday night and she was watching when I thought she was asleep. On Monday morning she was particularly excited by something she had seen and she started trying to tell me about it.'

As the woman talked, Isabella started to edge towards Peroni, still eyeing him as though he were a piece of lavish confectionary.

'At first I thought it was just the usual filth. A female was walking on the beach in the direction of the lighthouse from Piazza Nember when a man stepped out from the bushes and clasped her. They swayed backwards and forwards for some while as Isabella showed you and then they sank down together onto the sand.'

In spite of the growing interest the story aroused in him, Peroni was acutely aware of the fact that Isabella was now all but on top of him, her expression indicating she was about to devour him.

'Shortly after that,' the woman went on, 'the moon went behind clouds and when it came out again they had gone. But it was only today, when she was still talking about it, that I began to wonder whether it might not be something different from what I—and Isabella—had supposed it to be. The suddenness of it and the violence.'

The mongol girl was pressing herself against him now, and he was on the point of moving away when Signora Pizzini called her sharply, if belatedly off. She moved a couple of paces back as though a particularly toothsome delicacy had been snatched from her.

'And then I remembered the American girl and that according to the paper she must have been walking along just that stretch of beach at approximately the same time. So I brought Isabella to you.'

'Thank you,' said Peroni. 'Did she give you any idea what the girl was like?'

'She only said she was very pretty and had long, dark hair.'

'And the man?'

'Nothing.'

Questioning Isabella was impossible and there was nothing more to be learned from the mother so after a while, covering up as best he could the dull ache of dread within him, he thanked them and let them go.

Had it been Kehzia? And had the act been one of love or death? Either way there was little he could do about it except to make the already planned move.

Old Rita sat behind her stall, protecting herself as best she could from the assaults of the Bora dog which should return to its sky kennel sometime before tomorrow. From her shelter she studied the produce spread out for sale before her. If you half closed your eyes, the fruit and vegetables looked quite delicious; and as for the wine you didn't even have to do that; it was temptingly blood-red and golden in the necks of the flasks and nothing to show it was a little on the sharp side.

Only customers were lacking. Never frequent, they had

161

ceased altogether since the Bora had started blowing, and now it was getting dark as well. So, as the cash box was completely empty, she directed a quick prayer to her namesake, St Rita, the patron saint of the impossible, that one at least might come.

The speed with which St Rita could answer petitions was at times, so to speak, almost miraculous. So now. The prayer was scarcely out of her mouth when a car turned into the narrow road leading to her house and pulled up outside the stall.

As the customer got out she thought she had seen him somewhere before. Very handsome, southern looking, probably rich. She hoped that he would half close his eyes when he looked at the fruit and vegetables.

'*Buon giorno*,' he said. 'We've already met if you remember.'

'*Buon giorno*, your honour,' she said. An old customer. Now that was something to be proud of. 'What can I do for your honour?'

'You said you were born in Jesolo village?' said the customer.'

'That's right.' It was nice when they liked a bit of a gossip before making their purchases.

'And you can remember everything that happened when you used to live there?'

'Everything.'

'Does the name Zambelli mean anything to you?'

Zambelli. She closed her eyes and saw him at once. Old Signor Zambelli with his great big moustaches and hooked nose jutting out like a mountain peak and the eyes she had never had the courage to look straight into. 'He's dead now,' she said. 'They're all dead.'

'Iolanda Zambelli,' said the customer. 'Do you remember her?'

She closed her eyes again and saw Iolanda with her long black hair and full lips and beautiful teeth with the very slight gap between the two at the front. And she remembered the whole story. 'Sad it was,' she said. 'A sad way to die for a beautiful girl like that.'

'How did she die?' asked the customer.

She settled herself more comfortably and paused; she enjoyed

162

telling stories about the past. 'Old Signor Zambelli had a daughter,' she said, 'Iolanda. Now you have to understand, your honour, that things were different in those days. Oh, it was after the war and they'd started building Jesolo lido, but in Jesolo village people still thought and behaved as they used to do in the old days. Girls particularly—they wouldn't have dared even to dream of some of the things that girls get up to nowadays. Particularly Signorina Iolanda. Old Signor Zambelli was a strict man and a hard man. If he'd thought his daughter was up to something he'd have taken the strap to her, and left her more dead than alive, too. Oh, there was a young man in the village who was in love with her all right, but there wasn't much he could do about it beyond looking at her during Mass.

'But in Jesolo lido there were other ideas and ways of behaving coming in. Brought in by the tourists . . .'

She paused as an image came unbidden into her mind.

'You know the river Sile where it comes out into the sea by the lighthouse, your honour?' she said.

The customer nodded.

'It's bad there,' she said. 'Every year five or six people get drowned there, because where the river meets the sea there are strong currents. Well, that's what it was like in Jesolo then. You had the new ways coming in like the river at Jesolo lido and meeting the old ways at Jesolo village. That's what made it dangerous.

'One day a young American soldier who was on holiday at the lido came over to the village and he saw Signorina Iolanda and fell in love with her. What's more he got her to fall in love with him. Well, don't ask me how they did it, your honour, but they managed to outwit old Signor Zambelli. One or two people in the village knew about it, but he never suspected anything. And he wouldn't have done either, but after it was all over and the American had gone away she had to tell him that she was going to have a baby.

'There was a terrible scene. You could hear old Signor Zambelli shouting from one end of the village to the other. And when he'd done shouting he had her out of the house. Just like that with nothing but the clothes she stood in.

'Well, there was a rich family which had a villa outside the village and they took her in while she had the baby, and they'd have helped her afterwards to find herself a situation, too, but one night less than a week after the baby was born she drowned herself in the river at the bottom of the village.' She paused while her mind made the tedious journey back to the present.

'The American,' the customer was saying, and he seemed very excited, 'The American—can you remember anything about him?'

She had only seen him a couple of times in the street and that more than thirty years ago, and beyond the general impression that he was foreign looking she could remember nothing. 'No,' she said, 'no . . .'

'Try and think,' the customer begged her. 'Anything!'

She closed her eyes again in an effort of concentration because she didn't want to lose his good will, but she expected nothing and nothing came. 'No,' she said again, 'I'm afraid I can't.'

'Well, thank you anyway,' he said. 'You've been very helpful.'

And he turned back towards his car without buying anything. She looked reproachfully at the picture of the patron saint of the impossible: what was the good of bringing a customer if you let him go away without buying anything?

With his hand on the car door, the customer checked and turned. 'Oh, I forgot,' he said. 'I'll have six flasks of wine. Three red and three white.'

Joyfully she put them into two old cardboard boxes while he paid and then helped him carry them to the car and load them into the back. It was as she was straightening up painfully from this that something suddenly swooped into her mind like a seagull riding the Bora.

'There's just one thing I've remembered, your honour,' she said. 'about the American.'

He looked at her quickly. 'What's that?'

'His name. They called him Michele.'

With six flasks of vinegar in the back of his car, Peroni was driving along the narrow, deserted roads that crossed and intersected each other in the long stretches of insect-swarming fields and coppices behind Jesolo lido, scarcely noticing where he was going as he tried to follow all the possible implications to their utmost stretch. If the conclusions he had drawn were correct then somebody had linked up the events of more than thirty years ago with today. And then—

At this point in his thoughts a car started to cross an intersection in front of him so that he had to brake. Then for some reason the car stopped, completely blocking the road before him.

He was wondering why it should have done something so pointless when there was a sudden violent explosion behind him which sent him hurtling into his own windscreen and his car into the side of the one in front.

He just had time to realise that the apparent explosion had been caused by a third car crashing into the rear of his when he saw that men with stockings pulled over their heads and guns in their hands were emerging in what seemed like hordes from the two cars.

He reached for his own gun, but he was far too late. Two of the men were grabbing at him through the car door which had burst open in the crash and were pulling him out while somebody else struck him very hard on the back of the head with something that could have been Jesolo lighthouse. Peroni felt himself toppling into the dangerous vortex of waters where the river Sile meets the sea. And then he felt nothing at all.

The Captivity

Twenty-one

Television flicking was one of the children's more irritating habits. In Italy there are more private television companies than there are types of pasta, and Anna Maria and Stefano would run the gamut of all they could get. They were at it now, and it was driving her mad.

'Mamma taught me how to make my coffee irresistibly . . . start talking, buddie, or I'll . . . a beige two-piece ideal for . . . help! the monster's going to . . . Inter two, Juventus . . . the big time, honey, that's . . . small quantity of fertilizer on the . . .'

She was just going to scream at them to turn it off when she saw the title *Edizione Speciale TG2* appear on the screen.

'Leave it there,' she said. If there was a special bulletin at this hour, something unusual must have happened.

The newscaster was sitting behind his desk looking grave. 'Good evening,' he said. 'In a lightning operation just over an hour ago, the Free Jesolo Movement took over the Adriatic seaside town, announcing their intention of establishing it as an independent republic under the governorship of Captain Luigi Coliselli who made a previous bid for independence two years ago.

'The mayor of Jesolo, the head of police, leading town functionaries together with the proprietors of the principal hotels, land and property owners, have declared their loyalty to the republic and expressed one hundred per cent solidarity with the Free Jesolo Movement.

'Road blocks have been set up at the principal entrance points to the town and lido, but a spokesman for the Movement said that these are only temporary and it is hoped they will be removed in the immediate future. "The model for the Republic

169

of Jesolo," he added, "is San Marino not East Berlin." The spokesman also said that no harm will be done to holiday-makers, and all form of coercion will cease as soon as the Italian government has agreed to the independent status of Jesolo.'

The newscaster looked up from his sheet of paper. 'This news,' he said, 'has only just been received and confirmed. We hope shortly to have camera coverage of the *coup* and, at the same time, the official Italian government reaction.

'The news has come as a particular surprise in view of the fact that when Captain Coliselli made his original claim, it was generally held to be part publicity stunt and part local folk lore with no serious backing behind it. The story began when . . .'

As the newscaster continued to talk Assunta and her two children looked at each other in stunned bewilderment.

'It's been going on all around us, and we didn't even know!' said Stefano.

'Who would have thought something as exciting as this would happen,' said Anna Maria, 'and just when we can't go on the beach, too!'

'I'm going down to see what's happening,' said Stefano.

'Are you out of your mind?' said his mother. 'Do you want to be shot dead? Nobody's stirring from this flat!'

'But they said that no harm would be done to holiday-makers—'

'They can say what they like—you're staying here!'

'Let's have a look from the balcony at least,' said Anna Maria.

'Nobody's stepping out of this room,' said Assunta, 'until your Uncle Achille comes.'

At this point the telephone rang in the television studio. The newscaster coughed apologetically at the viewers and picked up the receiver. He listened for a moment nodding and saying, '*Si . . . Si . . .*' while his expression grew even graver.

'We've just received another communication purporting to come from the Free Jesolo Movement,' he said. 'The spokes-man, however, is different and refused to give his identity. He said that Commissario Achille Peroni, who was conducting an investigation at Jesolo, has been kidnapped and is being held hostage. If the demands of the Movement are not met by the Italian government within forty-eight hours, Commissario Peroni will be executed.'

Rock music *fortissimo*, the drums inside his head, pounding with steady, painful rhythm. He had no idea of where he was or even who he was. Nothing but the atrocious music.

And then, as painfully as if he were giving birth to himself, consciousness began to return. He knew who he was, but nothing else. Except that some disaster had befallen. And there was a vague sensation that he was on the brink of something important. But what? His mind stretched for it, found the effort too great and fell back into the blaring universe of rock.

But shortly after that it began to come of itself. Kehzia. Iolanda Zambelli and the American. Luca. It had all been pointing towards some solution when . . . The car stupidly braked in the middle of the intersection. The explosion. The men without faces.

Now he had compassed everything, but the process had been like undergoing major surgery.

He tried to open his eyes, but found he was unable to do so. Something was covering them; not just a bandage or a piece of cloth, but something that bit cruelly into the surrounding flesh. Sticking plaster. A mask of sticking plaster, applied so ruthlessly that not even a hint of light penetrated it. If there were any light.

The command went out from brain to hands that they should tear it off, but then he found that his hands were tied to something. And so, he realised a second later, were his feet. Something like the frame of a bed.

He was blind, powerless and totally ignorant of his circumstances. Including the time. There was no telling whether it was day or night. Or how long had passed since they had seized him. It could be an hour or a week. This total loss of the sense of time was almost as bad as the absence of sight; it was like suddenly finding oneself in outer space.

And the rock music screamed and throbbed relentlessly on, preventing any attempt at coherent thought.

171

Suddenly he realised that that was the purpose of it. Or one of the purposes.

He knew that in terrorist kidnappings rock music had a triple function. It facilitated brain-washing. It prevented the victim from getting any notion, via his sense of sound, as to where he was. And it could act as a sort of sonic camouflage for the prison itself.

But was this a terrorist kidnapping? Certainly it had all the hallmarks of one. Except that the terrorists chose their victims for carefully weighed political motives: in kidnapping Moro, Taliercio and General Dozier they had struck respectively at government, industry and NATO. But Peroni wasn't a key figure in the sense they were. So if not terrorists, who?

De Sanctis.

He had the money to organise such a kidnapping, and he must have been smarting badly as a result of Peroni's defection from the Satanist group. But would anybody in their right senses organise such a costly and complicated revenge for what was, after all, only a defection?

If it was only a defection.

All Peroni's doubts about motivation massed in a compact swarm. Supposing that he, Peroni, really, if unwittingly, had been on the track of something big at Jesolo. Something involving de Sanctis. That would explain the kidnapping. But if it were so, then what did de Sanctis intend doing next? As though an anaesthetic were beginning to wear off, fear began to prickle through his body.

And then suddenly the rock music stopped. His immediate thought was that it had somehow brought itself to a halt. But then it occurred to him for the first time that maybe he wasn't alone. He strained his ears for some other manifestation of whoever might be with him, but caught none. The silence was as terrifyingly all consuming as the music had been a minute before. And then out of it there came a voice.

'He's come round,' it said.

Peroni turned his head in its direction waiting for an answering voice, but none came so that he began to wonder whether the person could have spoken to himself. Then, just when he was almost convinced that he had a single guard, he heard the second voice speaking almost in his ear.

'How are you feeling, Commissario dear?' it said.

'How did it happen?' the President of Italy asked baldly.

'We don't know yet,' said the Mayor of Venice. 'It was totally unexpected. Everybody believed that the Free Jesolo Movement was a joke.'

'A very funny joke indeed!' grunted the President.

The two men were in a car speeding from the Marco Polo Airport through the village of Tessera and towards Venice.

The Mayor of Venice was a seasoned politician and a member of the Italian Communist Party since the tough old days when Togliatti had been party secretary, but even he was disconcerted by the present situation which had been made no easier by the President of the Republic's insistence on being personally present at the scene. 'Has this Coliselli man— Captain Gigi or whatever he's called—been arrested?' went on the President.

'No, Mr President,' the mayor admitted unhappily. 'An arrest was considered too dangerous. The Free Jesolo Movement is ostensibly playing this pacifically, but they're heavily armed and the place is full of tourists.'

'Pacifically!' snorted the President. 'Is kidnapping Peroni pacific?'

'Coliselli and the official organisers of the Movement claim they're not responsible.'

'Very probable! Who is responsible if not them?'

'Some unknown person or persons, they say, who stand to gain by the take-over.'

The President of Italy took off his glasses and pinched the bridge of his nose in a moment of silent suffering. He's beginning to realise, thought the mayor of Venice, that the Free Jesolo Movement has got us by the short and curlies.

'What's being done about Peroni?' continued the President after a minute.

'A police hunt was launched immediately—'

'What does immediately mean?'

173

'Unfortunately, nobody saw the kidnapping, Mr President. The hunt was started as soon as it was announced.'

'By the kidnappers themselves. So that Peroni was already in a carefully pre-selected prison. Do we have any indication of its locality?'

'The police believe it may be in Venice.'

'On what grounds?'

'It's a question of time, principally. Between when he was last seen late this afternoon and the announcement of the kidnapping early this evening there would have been just sufficient time to hide him in Venice.'

'Or somewhere along the Adriatic coast.'

'That is being searched, too.'

'And we have forty-eight hours to find him.'

There was no answer to that. The Mayor of Venice looked out of the window at the lowering, fire-spitting profile of Porto Marghera in the distance.

The voices were both male, but that was all they had in common. The one which had first spoken was rasping with a hint of cruelty, and Peroni had mentally dubbed its owner the butcher. The other could have belonged to a kindly male nurse, full of concern for his patient.

Peroni knew that both these men were his enemies, but in his blind and shackled circumstances this contrast in voices made him feel that the first was hostile while the second was friendly. So that already, before more than a few words had been spoken, a spider's web relationship was being woven in the air about them.

And then there were the smells. First there was an all-pervading musty smell which was the room itself and which suggested that they were in an old building. Then there was the smell of cooking: while he was unconscious his captors must have fried themselves some sort of meal. Thirdly there was the smell of cigarette smoke which was strong and made him feel the urge to smoke.

'Can I have a cigarette?' he asked.

'No,' said the butcher.

'Now why ever not?' said the male nurse.

'Because nobody said nothing about smoking.'

'Exactly. Nobody said he couldn't smoke.'

'Or that he could.'

'So there's no reason why he shouldn't have one.'

'Well, it's your responsibility.'

Peroni heard a cigarette being shaken from a packet, then felt it being placed between his lips. There sounded the light, grating sound of a lighter being lit.

'Draw, Commissario dear,' said the male nurse. It was hard to inhale without taking the cigarette out of your mouth. 'Sorry I can't undo your hands,' the nurse went on, 'but just nod when you want me to take the cigarette out.'

Peroni smoked, listening to the sounds about him. Breathing. The butcher's cigarette being put out in a tin ashtray, and then, almost immediately, another one being shaken out of a packet and lit. A page being turned. Not the page of a newspaper or a book. Something in between. A magazine.

Listening carefully, he could hear both men breathing. The nurse's breathing was soft and regular, and would have been altogether imperceptible if it hadn't been so near to him. The butcher's breathing was quicker and more laboured, almost panting.

Peroni nodded, and the cigarette was solicitously removed from his mouth. He heard the ash being shaken off, then felt the filter tip put gently once more between his lips.

Another page being turned over, but violently, almost wrenched, as though the butcher were desperate to see what was on the next page. And at the same time the sound of his breathing grew faster, heavier.

Then suddenly, as though the darkness had sharpened his inner perception, Peroni realised what was happening. The butcher was reading a pornographic magazine and moving rapidly towards an orgasm.

Confirmation of this came a few seconds later when the nurse said in a tone of disgust, 'Oh, put away that filthy magazine!'

There was no answer; just another page being wrenched over, a further acceleration of the breathing and then a long

175

shuddering groan.

'Really!' said the nurse.

The butcher continued to breathe hard, but now it was the breathing that follows on physical exertion and after a while there was the sound of yet another cigarette being lit.

Peroni's had burned down to the filter tip, and the nurse removed it delicately and stubbed it out. The smoke, he realised, had made him feel less listless so that, instead of making wild and nightmare stabs in the dark about his position, he became anxious to find out exactly what it was. Just how bad. But how to phrase the question? When you can't see your interlocutors, conversation is like walking through a room full of furniture in the dark.

'Who are you?' he asked, and realised at once that he had tripped over a verbal chair. 'I mean what organisation do you belong to?'

There was silence at this, and it lasted so long that Peroni began to wonder whether the two voices hadn't been aural delusions all along.

'Why don't you answer?' he said, understanding too late that he must sound as though he were pleading. And then he wondered whether the whole thing were not a deliberate cat and mouse game. If so, how could he stop himself being the mouse? Just keep silent, refuse to play the game. So he said nothing, and the butcher and the nurse were withdrawn into non-existence.

Peroni lay back in his darkness and listened to the silence. Even the breathing seemed to have stopped. Not a whisper, not a stirring. It could only be deliberate.

And then when the silence seemed to have lasted for at least an hour, the two voices started bickering again like an unexpected pattering of rain, and unpleasant though they were, they were a relief after the silence.

'Why not tell him?'

'Why should we?'

'We're not here to torture him.'

'We're not here to provide a walking information service either.'

'Why shouldn't he know?'

'They said not to communicate.'

'Unnecessarily.'

'This isn't necessary.'

'It's a question of humanity.'

'Humanity!' The butcher spat.

'Don't *do* that!' said the nurse, and the butcher laughed contemptuously.

'Don't worry, Commissario dear,' said the nurse as though to spite the butcher, 'we're not the Red Brigade. Nothing like that. We're the Free Jesolo Movement.'

The relief was almost unbearable. He forgot the ruthlessly organised kidnapping, the men with no faces, the mask of sticking plaster, and he just basked in this new awareness. He was held by what amounted to a light operetta political movement. Even the government at its most shilly-shallying could handle that. Rescue was surely imminent.

These thoughts flocked into his brain like the people of a town returning to their homes after a threat of general carnage has been lifted. To the sound of their footfalls Peroni relapsed again into unconsciousness.

Twenty-two

The hunt for Peroni was going on throughout Italy, but was particularly intense in Jesolo itself and in Venice. The Free Jesolo Movement and Captain Gigi claimed to have no knowledge of the Peroni kidnapping which they alleged was the work of another organisation. They had consequently made no attempt to interfere with the search there, and the sparse symmetry of the place was rendering this relatively easy. The same could not be said of Venice.

The Serenissima Republic is built on some hundred-odd islands and contains more bridges to the square mile than anywhere else on earth, rather more than four hundred and fifty which, as the diarist John Evelyn put it, "tack the city together". There are bridges of every shape and size, including one three-arched bridge and a labyrinthine junction of bridges near Piazzale Roma. There are more than three thousand alleyways and one hundred and seventy-seven canals, ranging from scarcely more than a sluggish trickle to the giant aquatic boa-constrictor which is the Grand Canal. There is a plethora of squares, some scarcely bigger than a telephone booth, with St Mark's—described by Napoleon as "the largest drawing room in Europe"—as their undisputed sovereign. And the buildings seem to have been scattered from some immense pepper-pot.

All this makes Venice one of the most devious urban jigsaw puzzles in the world and a nightmare to search. And the organisation of the search, which at first sight appeared to be of such computer-like exactitude that Peroni couldn't help being found well within the deadline if he were in Venice at all, was in fact a human, fallible and horribly chancy affair. They had to make selected swoops, and although the sites for these swoops were decided after careful consultation, they might just as well have been the result of tossing a coin. For every square metre examined, thousands were passed over.

And in less than forty-eight hours Peroni was to die.

'Well, I'm going to tell him!'

'No, you're not!'

'You told him who we were.'

'But this is different . . .'

The voices had penetrated Peroni's sleep so that at first he had thought they were part of a nightmare, but then the painful tautness of the sticking plaster and the rope cutting into his arms and ankles told him that he was awake again, though how long he had been unconscious he couldn't tell.

'He's got the *right* to know, hasn't he?' There was irony in the butcher's tone.

'Don't be silly!'

They were bickering as usual, but on different sides. Now it was the butcher who wanted Peroni to be told and the nurse who opposed telling him. Telling him what?

'He wanted to know how things stood, didn't he?'

'But it may come to nothing—'

'*Vacca!*' said the butcher. 'You want to bet on that?'

'But there's no *point* in telling him!'

'Yes, there is—I want to see his face when he hears.'

'We're here to guard him—not torture him.'

'Nobody said anything against a bit of torture.'

Peroni wondered tormentedly whether knowledge of what they were talking about could possibly be worse than the suspense he was now in. But he wasn't given the chance to choose. He felt himself being shaken roughly and the mixture of tobacco, alcohol and indigestion which was the butcher's breath on his face.

'Hey, policeman,' said the butcher. 'You want to know something?'

'Don't tell him!'

'If the government doesn't open negotiations with us, you're going to be shot!'

179

At that precise moment a telephone rang, as though to put its own shrill emphasis on the sentence of death. Momentarily it distracted Peroni from the contemplation of his own imminent death.

There was no reason why there should not be a telephone in the room, yet the sudden announcement of its presence at this moment could hardly have surprised Peroni more if it had been the trumpet sounding for the last judgement.

Its ringing jerked the entire situation violently upside down. An instant before, Peroni had been living in a closed world of three. From the moment he had regained consciousness after the kidnapping this world, inhabited only by himself and the two voices, had imposed itself on him and, little by little, he had come to accept it.

He, Peroni, blind and immobilised, was the centre of this world, and the butcher and the nurse moved about him, administering their smells, their touch, their emotions, the sound of their voices.

And now the sudden violent shrilling of the telephone had shattered the little world to pieces. Another character was about to be introduced.

Peroni heard the receiver being picked up.

'*Pronto?*' The nurse's voice was brittle with tension, and Peroni guessed that the telephone was only to be used in an emergency. '*Si . . . Si . . . Si . . .*' The thrice repeated monosyllable, sounding like the plucking of violin strings, confirmed Peroni's diagnosis of emergency. But what sort of emergency? Hope sprang painfully.

'*Si . . . Va bene . . . Subito . . .*' And the receiver was put down.

The words had given away nothing, but the tone had been eloquent, and the butcher, who now grunted an urgent interrogative, seemed as impatient as Peroni to know what had happened.

The answer was given him in the low, efficient whisper of a nurse conveying a serious message to the consultant in front of the patient, and Peroni felt a kick of irritation.

He strained to catch something of what was being said, but

the whisper was so infuriatingly discreet that he was unable to hook so much as a syllable.

Then the butcher said something and, although that was whispered, too, it wasn't so careful a whisper, and Peroni was able to pick out sounds here and there which could be unscrambled into words. There was something that sounded like 'here' and something else like 'away'. But the one that was clearest and best of all sounded very much indeed like 'police'.

And it must have been that, too, for when it was spoken there was a soft emphatic hiss as the nurse silenced the butcher before picking up once more his own urgent, inaudible whisper.

It wasn't a lot to go on, but taken in conjunction with the nurse's obvious state of tension, it could surely only be good. Police, taken on any reckoning, was hopeful. As for 'here' and 'away', they could well signify that the police were here and that Peroni and his guards must get away.

He was so absorbed in his speculations that he did not notice one of the two approach him. But now he felt the nurse's hand upon his arm and heard the nurse's voice in what sounded like a caricature of solicitude.

'Don't worry, Commissario dear,' it said. 'This isn't going to hurt. Just one tiny little prick and then you won't feel anything,'

Perez, the albino, and a DIGOS man who were part of a unit hunting for Peroni on the Giudecca, came to a bleak ancient house which seemed to be suffering from a perpetual streaming cold in its upper storeys as a result of having its foundations in the water for a couple of centuries. A couple of sitings of a furniture removal barge in a canal near this building were the immediate cause of their visit.

They entered the hall which was like an upturned Roman bath with two doors leading off it into apartments. Perez and his colleague tried the first one which was opened by a wizened, apple-cheeked old man who was cheerfully but helplessly drunk.

'*Questura*,' they said.

'Nolli, Giuseppe,' he said, giving his name and taking their hands in an affectionate clasp. 'Retired gondolier, ph'losopher,

lover 'v mankind 'n dialec' poet. Come in 'n have a shade of
wine and I'll read you a poem.'

They accepted the offer to come in, but declined the wine and
the poem.

'Have you noticed any movements at all unusual about here
last night or today?' they asked him without much hope.

'All the movements 'n this house 'r' unusual,' he said genially.
''S where I get my 'spiration from. 'S 'mazing the people that
come 'n go 'bout here.'

'For example?' said the DIGOS man irritably aware that he
was wasting his time.

'Oh, black men,' said the retired gondolier, collapsing more
or less accurately into a battered armchair, 'angels, a plumber
or two . . .'

Perez had been quickly examining the geography of the
apartment during these exchanges, and he now nodded to his
colleague who started for the door. '*Grazie, Signore,*' he said.

'Goin' already?' said the lover of mankind, standing with
difficulty and swaying backwards and forwards as though in a
high wind, 'Now *tha's* a pity! When I was 'joying the company
so much, too. 'Nother shade of wine?'

He insisted once again on taking their hands in a fondly
avuncular clasp. Then, when they had at last freed themselves
from this, they left the apartment and went to knock at the
other one on the ground floor.

The knock went unanswered, so they tried again. Still no
answer.

'Prob'ly busy unpacking,' came a familiar voice behind them.
Turning, they saw the philosopher clinging to his doorway and
blinking at them with undiminished geniality.

'Unpacking?' queried Perez.

'Tha's right,' said Nolli, Giuseppe, 'Saw 'em unloading a
'normous packing case las' night.'

'Unloading from what?' asked the DIGOS man sharply.

'Boat 'v course, my fine lad. 'S a canal round the back of that
'partment 'v theirs. Unloaded it straight in from the water
through the back door. Not f 'm a gondola 'v course. Gondola's
finest craft on God's earth. *La gondola xe la più bela cossa ghe*

182

Dio gh'abbia fato, but it wouldn't hold a packin' case 's big 's that.'

'What sort of boat did they have?' asked Perez, praying that the lucidity would hold out.

'Moval boat,' said the philosopher. He tried to give an idea of it by gestures, but without the hold of his hands on the door he started to topple dangerously, and the DIGOS man only just managed to catch him in time. 'Furn'ture boat,' he added, bestowing a grateful smile on his saviour.

With the old man still in his arms the DIGOS man looked at Perez and Perez at him.

'Who did the unloading?'

'People live in this 'partment 'v course.'

'And who are they?'

'Two fellers. Big one 'n lil one.'

'How long have they been here?'

'Only couple 'v weeks. Comin' 'n' goin' 't all hours. Painted Jez'bel stayed here before 'em—much more 'tresting . . .'

At which point he went right out, with a beatific smile at the thought of the painted Jez'bel.

Looking a bit like a gorilla with a sleeping infant un-expectedly dumped in its arms, the DIGOS agent carried the lover of mankind into his apartment, laid him on the bed and returned to Perez. They looked at each other again and the DIGOS man nodded almost imperceptibly.

Perez set to work. His fingers wove about the keyhole as delicately as a florist preparing a bouquet and within seconds the door fell open.

Guns ready, they crossed the small, dark entrance into a larger room, still dark and damp with flaking plaster on the walls. Cigarette smoke was heavy on the air and a smell of frying came from the tiny cubby-hole of a kitchen. But the apartment was indisputably empty and there was no trace of either a packing case or its contents.

Perez now went to the door opposite the entrance and found that it opened onto a stone mooring stage and a canal, just perceptibly licking its lips. No sign of a furniture removal barge.

Then they looked more carefully over the room. The DIGOS

man went to a low bed by one wall and found, on the floor by it, four pieces of rope which could have been used to tie somebody's wrists and ankles to the frame of the bed.

Perez went to a table at the other side of the room. There was a telephone on it, a cassette player with tapes of rock music and a large tin ashtray overflowing with cigarette stubs.

The telephone was a surprise. It was a new model, obviously recently installed, and it looked out of place in its surroundings.

Then Perez saw something which had fallen from the table. He stooped to pick it up and, when he had examined it for a second, gave a low whistle of surprise.

It was a photographic strip-cartoon magazine of hard-core porn.

The hunt shifted to the water. Police launches darted like purposeful dragonflies about the darkening expanse of the Giudecca canal, stopping every craft they found on it.

But some minutes before the police had taken to the water, a motor launch had chugged into a spacious water garage somewhere behind the Zattere and a group of people had helped the two men in it to unload a large packing case.

'We'll wait till later tonight,' said one of the group, 'then we'll shift him again, if possible before he regains consciousness. By land this time.'

Twenty-three

A middle-aged couple—he scrawny and bald, seemingly held
together by braces; she fat and bulging in pink Bermuda
shorts—were dancing frenetically in the middle of the tiny floor.
It was an absurd parody of pop dancing, a clumsy imitation of
their youngers which would have been funny if it hadn't been
pitiful. They were hopelessly drunk and laughed wildly as they
danced, apparently delighted at their own prowess.

They were watched by a large crowd which was clapping
rhythmically to the beat of the dance. Whether it was these
onlookers or the little orchestra which first started to accelerate
the pace there was no telling, but accelerate it did, and the
couple seemed compelled to follow it, like grotesque mario-
nettes being pulled by strings.

They stopped laughing, but seemed unable to stop dancing.
Faster and faster they went, staggering more and more wildly
about. And still the music and the clapping continued to
accelerate until it seemed as though the floor were heaving
beneath them as if in an earthquake.

And then at last the woman collapsed. There was wild
applause at this, though whether for the spectacle or its abrupt
termination it was impossible to tell. She lay on the floor with
her fat legs wide open, and somebody's hand inserted the neck
of a champagne bottle into her wide open mouth.

The camera moved in for a close-up of the bottle and then out
again for a wide shot of the onlookers and the orchestra. It
might have been a classical painting of a Bacchanalian orgy if
all the participants hadn't been so hideous to look at.

'As you can see,' said the television commentator, 'the
takeover of this Adriatic seaside town last night by the Free
Jesolo Movement has done nothing to diminish the high spirits

of holiday-makers. Indeed, quite the contrary. Many hotel and restaurant owners have provided free champagne to celebrate what they describe as the inauguration of Jesolo as an independent republic.'

Peroni's sister and her two children were sitting in front of the television. It was torment to watch, but it would probably have been worse torment to switch off and speculate.

Assunta looked at her watch.

'Less than twenty-four hours to go,' she said.

'Less than twenty-four hours to go,' said the Prefect of the Venetian region.

'I'm aware of that!' said the Mayor of Venice who was getting edgy. The President of the Republic was not present at the meeting, but he was sitting in his suite at the Danieli hotel waiting for hourly reports. And for results.

'We can't allow him to be killed while it's in our power to save him!' said the Prefect.

'And we can't bargain with criminals!' snapped the Mayor.

Dott. Amabile closed his eyes in silence. This was where they had been heading ever since the meeting—held in the largest room in the Venetian municipal palace and attended by all the city and regional authorities—had begun over an hour before. For this was the great fundamental issue that arose every time a man's life was at stake as a result of criminal blackmail.

They had started off common-sensically enough, dealing practically with the multifarious problems concerned with the hunt for Peroni whose prison, they were as certain as ever they could be, was not in Jesolo where a building-by-building search had been completed earlier that evening. But now they were soaring towards those dangerous regions of emotion and ideology where few Italians can keep their heads.

'You say that, Mr Mayor,' the Prefect snapped back, 'because it is *now* the Communist Party line to oppose negotiations in such cases. It seems to me inhuman that a man should be killed to preserve a party political line!'

'It is indeed the Communist Party line to oppose such negotiations,' shouted the Mayor over the uproar that had

186

exploded at the Prefect's remark, 'and in other circumstances I should be quite prepared to defend that line. This evening, however, no defence is necessary. The government itself has firmly rejected any possibility of negotiations.'

'A flat refusal is tantamount to abandoning Peroni!' said the Prefect. 'It's unthinkable that a civilised, democratic country should even consider abandoning one of its citizens. Still less one of its most deserving citizens.'

'There is nobody in this room,' said the Mayor, 'who does not feel acute anguish for the Commissario. But the fact remains that to negotiate with the Free Jesolo Movement would open the way to a hijacking of cities throughout Italy. It would be a return to the dark ages with the country divided into an endless series of city states!'

Within the cloud of pipe smoke that enveloped his upper reaches, *dott.* Amabile took leave to wonder whether anybody in that room felt acute anguish for Peroni; he himself was the only person who even knew him personally.

He also wondered how much longer the meeting could possibly last.

Volare, oh—oh
Cantare, oh—oh—oh—oh . . .

Although she knew perfectly well she was no Callas, Ornella usually enjoyed her singing. But not tonight. And not last night either.

Ever since she had heard the news of the kidnapping of Commissario Peroni and the threat to murder him, singing had been about as enjoyable as forced vomiting.

It was nearly midnight now, and the Dolce Vita still gave no signs of closing. Everybody—waiters, holiday-makers, Maurizio and his band and King Bag-of-Guts himself—was hell-bent on enjoyment, laughing like a Hell-full of lunatics, flushed and somewhere between ninety-nine and one hundred per cent roaring drunk.

With the human sacrifice demanded by their oh – so – wonderful *festa* waiting somewhere to be shot.

187

Nel blu dipinto di blu,
Felice di stare lassu . . .

And the worst of it was that Ornella felt herself in some vague way responsible. She couldn't think how or why this should be, but there had been something decidedly odd about that trip the last time she had seen him. He had looked worried to death and then, just after Igor Stravinsky, he had broken away almost violently and said he must go back to Jesolo. She had assumed that she had once again said the wrong thing to the right man, but now she began to wonder. Could she somehow have said something that set him off on the path leading to imprisonment and death?

And if so, what?

But no, it wasn't the moment for asking questions like that. This wasn't one of those things that squared logically. This was instinct: the instinct that a lot of men laughed off as women's, putting it on a par with old wives' tales. And Ornella believed in the reliability of her feminine instinct, as she believed in lots of old fashioned things like love and home-made pasta and her guardian angel. So if her instinct told her she was somehow responsible for Peroni's predicament she believed it.

So? Well, for one thing it wasn't enough for her to stand up there singing to a lot of moronic drunks. It was up to her to do something.

But what?

Several thousand men were engaged in looking for Peroni. Helicopters were scanning the length and breadth of Italy. There were road blocks, dragnets, swoops, house-to-house searches, random checks. And with all this going on she believed that she, Ornella Campana, fourth rate nightingale in a fifth rate floorshow, could somehow do something?

Yes, as a matter of fact she did.

But the question still remained, what?

She glanced at her watch. Quarter to midnight. That meant the next song was her last. The rest of them could drink, dance, eat and shout themselves into well deserved graves if they wished. But she would be free to go home. And to think.

188

Nel blu dipinto di blu came to an end, and it was time for the last song. Ornella looked at her now howling and besotted public and reflected that it would make little difference to them if she sang the *Ring* cycle or the telephone directory. But she would sing neither. She would sing what she always did sing last of all.

She would sing *Arrivederci Roma*.

One of the oldest of human nightmares had come true for Peroni. He had been buried alive. He could feel himself hemmed in by the lid, sides and bottom of the coffin. Strange he couldn't remember when they had shot him, stranger that he could feel no effects of the shooting, but that was little consolation when he was to die the far crueller death of suffocation in the grave.

But then he realised with sudden relief that he could breathe with relative ease, the air about him being stale but abundant. And something else: his coffin was moving. He could feel a slight jolting and catch the sound of an engine. He was in some sort of vehicle.

The awareness of this brought back his last conscious memories in a rush, and he understood with piercing despair that the police had indeed been on the brink of discovering his prison and that his captors had succeeded in moving him in time.

And then he realised that the vehicle in which he was being transported was slowing down. Slowing down and stopping. So the effects of the injection had worn off before the transfer to his new prison had been completed. Maybe then he could get a clue as to its whereabouts. He strained his faculties in the hope of catching some tiny giveaway sound.

Silence as the engine was turned off. Somebody quite near shifting their position. More silence: a disconcerting amount of it, broken eventually by the sound of a door (a van door?) being opened somewhere behind his head.

A grunt. Not much, but enough to tell him that the butcher was still around.

Then he felt his mobile coffin being slid back and jerked upwards. He was obviously being carried, and a faint oily smell

189

suggested he was in a garage.

Another door opening. Steps upwards. One, two, three . . . He counted up to twelve before they straightened out again and started walking along what might have been a corridor.

And then a sudden freshness suggested they were passing a half open window. Something giving a crack onto the world outside his new prison. And through it, miraculously, he caught the sound he had been straining for. Brief, faint, distant, but unmistakable: the sound of a voice he knew.

'*Arrivederci Roma*,' it sang, 'Goodbye, goodbye to Rome . . .'

Ornella caught a bus as far as Piazza Marina from where it was only a short distance to the house where she lived with her mother. But the road was still weaving with besotted revellers, so she preferred to cut down to the sea and walk along the beach.

The Bora had finished its three-day tumble and Jesolo was having a spell of the perfect weather which sometimes comes towards the end of September. The sea, lapping tenderly at the end of the jetties, stretched out in black velvet towards Yugoslavia while the moon threw across it a defiantly chocolate box highway of silver.

Almost without being aware she was doing so, Ornella took off her shoes and started to walk along the foreshore, swinging them in her left hand as she went and pursing her lips in a soundless whistle which was a habit of hers when thinking.

The feeling that in some inexplicable way she had a finger in the pie of Peroni's destiny was nagging at her more and more insistently. But what she might do to alter its present course was no clearer.

She walked to the end of a jetty and, as there was nobody about, lay down on her tummy to listen to the whispering of the sea as she used to do as a little girl (and the hell with her long Dolce Vita dress, she thought as she lay).

She would have liked to ask *la mamma* for advice, but this particular problem was a bit beyond *la mamma's* scope, so she turned to the sea instead. After all, the sea was meant to be maternal, wasn't it?

She poured the problem out in concentrated thought and lay there, half imagining she could see it spreading on the smooth surface like oil and then slowly being absorbed by the water until it had vanished below the surface.

There was a pause as though the sea were reflecting and then the whisperings below her began again. Ornella listened carefully, her fair hair falling about her face towards the water, and after a while it seemed to her that she could make out words, the purport of which she was not slow in grasping.

The sea had come up with an idea all right. Though not, Ornella couldn't help reflecting, the sort of idea she might have expected from *la mamma*.

Twenty-four

There was an electronic clock in the operations centre of the Venetian *Questura* which worked, unlike most things there, with one hundred per cent precision. *Dott.* Amabile hated it. He would have preferred something with a grubby face bearing the maker's name, sweeping hands, a loud tick and a tendency to lose at least five minutes a day. Instead he had to live with this impassive electronic monster.

He had never hated it so much as now. It said three forty-seven and twenty-two seconds. Twenty-three seconds. Twenty-four seconds. Given the fact that the Free Jesolo Movement had issued their ultimatum at eight p.m. two days previously this meant that Peroni had exactly four hours, thirteen minutes and thirty-six seconds to live.

Thirty-five seconds.

Thirty-four seconds.

Assuming that the Free Jesolo Movement was as accurate as that *maledetto* electronic clock.

The most massive police hunt had been mounted since the one following the Moro kidnapping, but all it had found so far was Peroni's prison—a good half hour after Peroni had been moved from it. And the subsequent ransacking of every craft in the city from gondolas to liners had produced nothing. Peroni had been spirited away as efficiently the second time as he had the first.

Four hours, thirteen minutes and twelve seconds.

One of the telephones on Amabile's desk rang.

'*Pronto?*'

'There's a man on an outside line, *dottore*, who says he can trace *dott.* Peroni.'

'Put him through.'

There was a click and the volunteer was speaking. 'Is that the *Questore*?'

'*Si.*'

'I have an infallible system for finding Peroni. It consists of a magic pendulum which, after being wrapped in some article of a person's clothing and then swung over a map of Italy will come to rest over the city or area where that person is. The swinging is then repeated over a large scale map of the city or area indicated and the person's whereabouts are then clearly revealed. I am prepared to put this system at the service of the police in exchange for five million lire to cover my expenses . . .'

Gently, with an expression which revealed nothing, *dott.* Amabile put the receiver back on its cradle.

Four hours, twelve minutes and twenty-six seconds.

He was in Jesolo.

But this information, gained against odds which could only be calculated in terms of light years, was utterly useless. It also spawned yet more despair. For Jesolo must have been the first place to have been searched, building by building, while he was in his other prison. And the police would not be returning to ground they had already covered.

After that fleeting sound of *Arrivederci Roma*, he had been taken into a room and uncoffined. Then the nurse, with horrible solicitousness had looked after his bodily needs, and Peroni had had some salami and goat's milk cheese with coffee.

His fitful sleep was riddled with nightmares until the nurse made coffee again, and he guessed it must be morning.

His last morning.

Now he had lost all count of how long had passed since the coffee; it could have been hours or minutes. The butcher sounded as if he had gone asleep and the nurse, having found a pack of cards, was playing patience.

With no particular aim in mind, Peroni flexed his ankles and feet and discovered, without particular interest, that the rope had left him a small amount of play with his left hand. Not enough to mature into action; not enough to be of any significance whatsoever; just a very small amount of play with

193

one hand.

He used it to its fullest stretch in both directions and found after a few minutes that he could increase the play slightly. Never to the extent of undoing the knot, but he could gain a few centimetres and, he discovered, just touch the wall beside the bed.

It was some sort of wooden panelling. He explored as much of it as he could with his fingers and found a crack. This was painful as the rope cut into his wrists, but the effort somewhat took his mind off the situation and there was a small, futile sense of achievement in getting his nail into the crack.

It was when he had done this that he realised the panelling was loose.

This could be of no conceivable help to him. Even if he did the impossible and pried it free, he was still bound and blind. But he determined to try in spite of this.

The first, fine, careless rapture of his new status was beginning to pall, and Captain Gigi was feeling a hint of uneasiness. What if things went wrong? The power behind him was considerable, but was it strong enough to outface the Italian government in a battle of wills? What if things went wrong?

And what if they went right? For the first time he began to feel a certain uneasiness about that, too. He knew he was a puppet, and the idea of being manipulated by the power that held his strings did not appeal to him.

Perhaps the reason for this growing sense of depression and anxiety was that he was alone. It was late afternoon, and the revellers who had helped to keep him in a state of euphoria till then had either gone or passed out. The weather didn't help either, for it was getting dark and chilly outside and he could feel the approach of autumn.

The media people had gone, too, and he wondered uneasily whether the government might have come to an agreement with them to ignore the whole business in an attempt to suffocate it by silence.

Captain Gigi sat alone, bloated, bloodshot and flaccid, in the darkening back room of the Dolce Vita, imagining for himself sad stories of the death of kings. He was badly in need of a little consolation.

'Good evening, Captain Gigi.'

The voice was the last he had been expecting to hear, and he looked, blinking, in the direction from which it came, wondering what it might portend.

Two hours, twelve minutes and thirteen seconds.

Dott. Amabile had never felt frustration in his career so painfully before. His position obliged him to stay in the *Questura* co-ordinating the hunt for Peroni, sifting through the flood of information, reports, suggestions, false alarms which was by now pouring in from all over Italy, but he would gladly have sacrificed his now imminent pension to be taking an active part in the search.

He glanced with a stirring of academic irritation at the newspaper on his desk. PERONI TO DIE? said the biggest headline he had ever seen, *All police efforts to trace the Wizard of Naples so far in vain.*

The publicity, Amabile reflected wryly, would have given Peroni great satisfaction. If only he had been able to see it.

Two hours, eleven minutes and fifty-seven seconds.

Prising open the panel without his captors' knowledge had become the centre of Peroni's existence. If he had been unbound and unobserved, the job would have taken less than a second. As it was he already seemed to have been engaged on it for ever.

From the various sounds coming from the nurse and the butcher he had calculated their position as nearly as he could, and he had guessed that the movement of his left hand was hidden from them by his body. Naturally he had to make this movement as slight as possible and stop it altogether when anything suggested they might be looking in his direction.

The extreme restriction of movement made even the slightest distances seem enormous, and the fact that his entire forefinger was now in the crack when he had started with only a finger-nail seemed a conquest comparable to that of Everest.

He suspected, too, that the panel was hollow, and the entire force of his curiosity was concentrated on discovering if this were so.

A few minutes more, and his finger would be through the woodwork and into the space behind. If there was a space behind.

'Commissario dear,' came the voice of the nurse from unexpectedly close. 'What are you doing with the wall?'

'Good evening, Captain Gigi.'

Making her voice sound friendly was about the biggest effort Ornella had ever made in her life, but it must have been successful for satisfaction seemed to take the place of surprise on his repulsive, moon-like face.

'*Ciao*, Ornella,' he said. 'Drink?'

I'd rather die of thirst than drink with you, thought Ornella. 'Thanks,' said Ornella, 'I'll have an Aperol.'

'Drop of gin in it?'

I know what your offers of gin mean, you fat louse, thought Ornella. 'Thanks,' said Ornella. 'Just a drop.'

Wobbling with excitement he went off to the bar while she followed him with a look that should have melted his rolls of flesh into so much snail-slime.

She looked quickly at her watch. She hadn't been able to get him alone before, and now it was late. And the worst of it was that she dared not hurry; the project was risky anyhow, but the slightest haste would ruin it altogether.

He returned with two glasses and, as she had expected, the bottle.

'Here we are,' said Captain Gigi, pouring ample gin into the Aperol. 'Chin chin!'

I hope it chokes you, thought Ornella. 'Chin chin', said Ornella. 'What's it like being governor of Jesolo?'

'Not all it's cracked up to be, my dear.'

That "my dear", thought Ornella, had all the delicacy of a hand being slapped on your bottom. 'How's that?' she said in what she hoped was a sympathetic tone.

'Well, for one thing it's the uncertainty. How's it all going to end? And then there are—other worries, too.'

'For example?' she said. 'I mean only if you want to tell me, of course.'

'Have another drop of gin?'

'If you'll join me.'

He poured ample measures for both of them, and although Ornella detested gin almost as much as she detested Captain Gigi she was not altogether displeased; it might speed things up. She downed hers quickly and tried not to shudder.

Captain Gigi apparently took this for abandonment for he poured her another and then, a second later, she felt something like a fat fish landing upon her knee and then starting to squirm as though it had just been caught. She edged her chair away.

'Why don't you like being governor?' she asked.

'It's lonely,' he said looking profoundly sorry for himself.

I might have expected he'd pull that one out of the hat, thought Ornella; next thing he'll be telling me nobody understands him.

'And nobody understands me!'

Oh, mio Dio! Are there no depths he won't sink to? 'You're not lonely now, Gigi. I'm with you. And I understand you.'

'Do you, Ornella? Do you really?' He poured more gin for them, and she was horrified to see two large tears oozing out of his piggy eyes. 'You know, I've always thought, Ornella is the only one who could understand me.'

'I'm glad you feel like that, Gigi.' The fish arrived back again, and she supposed she'd better let it stay this time.

'I do, Ornella—truly I do!'

The sorrier he is for himself, she thought, the more worked up he gets. If it wasn't horrible, it would be funny. *Oh, mio Dio,* that fish! I must just keep on thinking I'm doing it for Commissario Peroni. 'Tell me more about it, Gigi.'

'Shall we go upstairs? I'll tell you there.'

'Upstairs?'

'I just mean we can be more private there.'

If you think I don't know what you just mean, you're even stupider than I took you for.

'Shall we go then, Ornella?'

I don't think I can go through with this even for Commissario Peroni. 'Yes, Gigi, let's go.'

197

Twenty-five

'Commissario dear, what are you doing with the wall?'

Too late Peroni withdrew his forefinger from the crack in the panelling. His sense of hearing had let him down altogether about the nurse's approach and now, absurdly, he was flooded with a bitter sense of failure.

'Found a crack, have you?'

'Trying to escape?' said the butcher.

'Oh, dear me, no!' said the nurse with a giggle, 'Don't be so silly—he knows very well he couldn't do that! He was just curious, weren't you, Commissario dear?'

Peroni felt a body leaning over him and heard knuckles tapped against the panelling.

'Well, fancy that!' came the nurse's voice. 'It's hollow! So of course you were curious, weren't you? I'm curious, too. Let's have a look see what's inside.'

'You can't do that!' interrupted the butcher. 'It's not our place.'

'Oh, pooh! I'm only taking away a little bit of panelling. We can easily put it back afterwards, can't we?'

'What if they find out?'

'They wouldn't even *care*, silly!'

'Well, it's your responsibility.'

'Of course it's my responsibility. Hang on a minute—we'll soon have it open.'

Peroni again felt the nurse leaning over him and then heard the sound of splintering wood.

'Ooh!' exclaimed the nurse. 'It's a tiny little cubby-hole. What a *thrill*! Somebody must have taken the panel away and then removed some bricks before putting it back. And there's something inside! I hardly dare touch it!'

198

'Oh, go on—don't be so stupid!'

'Shall I? Well, I suppose it won't bite me, will it? Shall I be brave, Commissario dear? Yes, I will.' There was a pause and then another squeaky 'Ooh! It's a box,' went on the nurse, 'a tin box. We'll take it over to the table and see if it opens.'

Peroni heard the nurse going away and the box being placed on the table.

'No, it's not locked,' said the nurse. 'Now let's see what's inside.' There was a pause followed by a bawdy chuckle from the butcher. 'Don't be nasty,' said the nurse, 'I think it's very sweet. You know what it is, Commissario dear? It's a girl's box of keepsakes. Some girl who lived here quite a long time ago I should think—to judge by what's inside. There's a faded rose and a little ring—isn't that pretty now?—and some ribbons and a mother-of-pearl brooch—oh, and a letter. I don't think we can read that, can we? Like prying into the poor girl's private life. I think we'll just put it back.'

'Oh no, you won't!'

'Yes, I will!'

There was the sound of a brief scuffle, and then Peroni heard a grunt of triumph.

'Now then,' said the butcher, 'we'll have ourselves an earful of the young lady's sex life.'

'I shan't listen!' said the nurse.

'Please yourself,' said the butcher and then paused as though taking up a comical stance for the reading. 'My dearest Iolanda,' he began in a mock amorous voice.

For a split second Peroni wondered where he had heard the name before. Then he remembered and, in spite of his predicament, stiffened with interest.

'My dearest Iolanda,' went on the butcher, 'Those moments we were able to get alone together in church this morning were the happiest of my life. The ring you gave me I will treasure as my dearest possession for the rest of my life. I know that it will be very difficult for us to marry because of your father, but I will wait in hope for the rest of my life if necessary because I would sooner die than marry somebody else—'

'Oh, stop it!' squealed the nurse. 'It really isn't nice!'

199

'What, stop now?' said the butcher. 'Just when we're getting to the dirty bit? Stuff your ears if you don't want to listen, and the Commissario and me'll hear how she got something else stuffed.'

He shook with laughter at this witticism and then resumed his comic reading. 'Your beauty, my dearest Iolanda, is with me night and day. However miserable I may be, I have only to close my eyes to see your beloved face—your eyes shining with all the brightness of love, your soft lips, your sweet nose, your wonderful long black hair. Goodnight, goodnight, my beloved Iolanda. I love you, I love you, I love you now, tomorrow and for ever!'

Having reached his comical climax, the butcher paused before reading out the name at the foot of the letter. As he did so, Peroni saw in his darkness a blinding flash that was at the same time both triumph and despair.

He knew now that Kehzia had been killed. He knew why she had been killed. And he knew who had killed her.

The information had reached him in the one situation of his life when he was powerless to do anything about it. And likely to remain so for eternity. If the White Lady had come for him at last, she would surely carry him out on the most ironical situation of his existence.

Then, as though to emphasize the probability of this, there came a sudden stiffening of tension in the room and the butcher said, 'Here, put that stuff away! That's their car stopped outside. They must have come to—'

'Shh!' the nurse interrupted in a flustered voice. 'Don't be tactless!'

Fifty-eight minutes and twenty-two seconds to go.

From within his cloud of pipe smoke, *dott*. Amabile was observing every movement made in the operations centre, even those apparently behind his back, and he noticed immediately when a policewoman's expression flashed with sudden interest as she took a radio message.

'What is it?' he asked as soon as she had finished copying.

'They've found a furniture removal barge in an abandoned

garage on the Giudecca, *dottore*,' she said. 'They think it was used to transport *dott.* Peroni.'

'*Grazie, Signorina*.' The polite words were, as usual, impeccable, but there was a weariness in Amabile's voice as he spoke them. The discovery was important, of course, but there was no concealing the fact that they were still at least one step behind in the pursuit.

'Dear Minister,' Amabile found the words forming uncalled for within his mind. 'Under the circumstances I have no alternative but to offer my resignation. As *Questore* of Venice I must accept full responsibility for the failure to trace *dott.* Peroni in time . . .'

He shook the words irritably away and looked with dislike at the implacable electronic clock.

Fifty-six minutes and thirty-nine seconds.

Captain Gigi had a nasty attack of hiccoughs as a result of too much gin, but in spite of this he was feeling pleased with himself. Not so much because of Ornella's surrender, but rather because he had found in her the mamma he had so long been looking for. Her sympathy had called forth that plump little Gigi who lurked within the Captain's flabbily mountainous exterior.

'Mamma,' he now murmured, nudging her and feeling her stiffen with delight at his side, 'Hic!'

'Who's a naughty little boy who's had too much gin?'

'Gigi. Mamma smack naughty Gigi.'

To his delight she smacked him—to tell the truth a little harder than he had bargained for—on one of his monumental buttocks.

'Now,' she said when the chastisement was for the moment over, 'Mamma wants Gigi to tell her all his worries. You promised remember.'

And that was a source of pleasure to him, too. Ever since the business started he had been yearning for a maternal ear into which he could pour his troubles, and now at last he had one.

'Gigi's worried,' he said, 'that it'll all—hic!—go wrong. Gigi's worried that they'll put him in prison!'

'Why should it all go wrong, you silly little boy?'

'Well, for one thing when they've shot that policeman, they won't—hic!—have anything left to bargain with.'

'*If* they shoot him, Gigi. Maybe the police'll find him first.'

'Oh no, they won't.'

'How can you be so sure?'

'Because Gigi knows—hic!—where he's hidden.'

'Mamma doesn't believe *that*—Gigi's telling naughty fibs.'

'No, he isn't!'

'Yes, he is!'

'No, he isn't! They keep Gigi in touch with what's—hic!— happening!'

'Mamma still doesn't believe it.'

'I'll tell you where he is then!'

'Mamma isn't interested.'

'He's in—hic!—Jesolo. He's in the very house opposite where we are now!'

'Mamma isn't listening!'

'And the police'll never think of coming here because they've searched the whole place already.'

'Mamma's going to smack Gigi again for telling silly stories.'

'No!' said Gigi, turning obediently onto his tummy, 'Please mamma! Gigi won't do it again. Hic! Ow!'

Twenty-six

Peroni's executioner had come into the room.

If any communication was passing between him and the two guards it could only be by looks, for there was total silence which seemed to go on for a long time. This was eventually followed by the sound of feet and of the door opening and closing for the second time. And then of one person moving towards him and halting.

Peroni tensed himself for the sudden blast of a bullet which would leave him suddenly shelterless before the great wind of eternity. And as there was no time for complicated negotiations with his maker, he put the whole business fair and square into the hands of St Janarius.

But the expected blast did not come. Instead the silence protracted itself impossibly like a piece of chewing gum stretching out indefinitely. Peroni had the impression that the executioner was standing immediately over him. But was the silence gratuitous torture or was he, for some mysterious reason, being studied?

And then he caught something that took him a micro-instant to identify.

The smell of Pernod.

He was in no doubt now as to who was standing over him, and the shock was almost as shattering as a bullet. He had always thought of the Free Jesolo Movement as a separate compartment, absurd, anachronistic, deadly, but a thing unto itself. And yet there could be no mistaking that smell.

And then, in confirmation of it, came the voice. 'Why did you renege?' it said.

Peroni knew that the story of St Janarius and Ornella just wouldn't take with de Sanctis and he had nothing else to say, so

203

his silence was not heroic. Yet he had the odd impression that momentarily it seemed to give him the upper hand.

'You renounced all we could have given you,' went on de Sanctis as though the words were being squeezed out of him by Peroni's non-reply, 'in exchange for this.' And Peroni heard a gun being cocked somewhere near his right ear.

There still seemed to be no answer, so he tried a question instead. 'So you're the brains behind the Free Jesolo Movement?'

'We are.'

'What's it all about?'

'You might say—a slight case of infection.'

'I'm not with you.'

'Satanism is the most powerful force on earth, Commissario, and it's infectious. *You* know that. You felt it that evening, whatever may have happened to you subsequently. So why then has it always been so restricted?'

In the pause left by the rhetorical question Peroni realised that de Sanctis was more than slightly drunk, and he wondered, desperately, whether that might be cause for hope.

'Why have its adherents always been exceptional or warped or eccentric? Why has it never caught the imagination of ordinary people? We thought about this for a long time and eventually we came to a very simple conclusion. Satanism has never possessed any territory—ordinary territory onto which large numbers of ordinary people regularly converge. If we could own some land like that, we thought—it need be no bigger than the Vatican State or the Republic of San Marino— and give the necessary key positions in it to our own people, it would be easy to reach and sway the affections of the people who came there.'

There's something wrong, thought Peroni; apart from the sheer lunacy of the whole thing, there's something that doesn't quite square up, but I can't think what it can be.

'But how would you go about reaching and swaying the affections of people, as you put it?'

'People are vulnerable when they're on holiday. Their minds are open to anything that offers itself. They've also got a lot of time on their hands, and they're ready for adventures they wouldn't embark on in the course of their ordinary lives. If somebody towards the end of a genial evening were to initiate a ceremony such as the one you attended, a holiday maker would scarcely be likely to withdraw. After all, he would see it as no more than a slightly exotic pastime.'

He likes talking, thought Peroni. Put together with the amount of Pernod he's drunk, that might just add up to something. Keep him fuelled with questions.

'Granted that,' he said, 'but still it's surely a long way from a little holiday table-turning to making any notable inroad with humanity?'

'You know the story about the king who placed a single grain of corn on the first square of a chess board, double the quantity on the second square, doubled it again on the third and so on, until by the end he discovered that the amount of corn vastly outweighed all the granaries of his kingdom? That's how it'll be. We can expect several hundred initiates in a season. Once initiated it is almost impossible to withdraw, and at the same time the initiate himself feels a more and more irresistible urge to gain more adherents. At that rate it wouldn't be slow in reaching gigantic proportions.'

'But the truth would get out,' Peroni objected.

'Eventually,' de Sanctis agreed, 'but by then we should have achieved our objective and there would be neither harm nor danger in proclaiming ourselves openly. But until then Jesolo would remain Captain Gigi's republic, slightly absurd, but charming and romantic. For that's how we shall make it, Commissario. Jesolo at the moment isn't notable for either charm or romance, but it will be when we've done with it. There'll be no end to the flags and coloured lights and dashing uniforms and love songs—all presided over by Captain Gigi, the embodiment of geniality and good cheer. Already holiday-makers come here from almost all over the world, so how much more then. It's odd to think that from such an operetta-like little republic should spring the first capital of the Kingdom of Satan on earth, isn't it? And it's a pity that you can't be a part of it, Commissario. You would have been a great asset—that's why I invited you to dinner that night. I've wanted you to be one of us.'

'And Kehzia?' he said. 'Why did you involve her?'

The answer came after a pause in a sudden roar of pain. 'I loved her!'

'And so you killed her?'

'I never killed Kehzia!'

Peroni knew this was correct, but an instinct told him that playing on de Sanctis's nerves was the ideal system for procrastinating.

'You're lying, de Sanctis!'

But he had miscalculated, and for answer what could only be a gun barrel was jammed hard into his rib-cage roughly in correspondence with the heart.

It had come off in both senses of the word, though Ornella with a vulgarity of phrase she would normally never have permitted herself, but which under the circumstances she felt more than justified. If only now it wasn't too late!

Getting away was the first problem. To abandon him immediately she had learned of Peroni's whereabouts might have ruined everything. So she had to allow his depraved and whale-like heavings to reach a temporary conclusion. Then, dodging his grabbing arms as best she could and saying that mamma had to go shopping for Gigi's din-dins, she somehow managed to get away and down the stairs.

The next problem was finding a telephone. There was one in the Dolce Vita, but she didn't dare use that and, with Peroni held captive right opposite, she thought it would be risky to use any of the 'phones in the immediate vicinity. But where else was there one?

Her mind made a lightning review of the geography of Jesolo village in search of a public telephone far enough away from the Dolce Vita.

Somewhere in the direction she had come from there was a sharp explosion. She halted as though the bullet had struck her, and then realised it was only the back-firing of a car.

But where, oh where, could she find a telephone?

Miraculously the trigger wasn't pulled and Peroni hauled himself cautiously back on to the cliff-edge of existence. 'Why did you choose Jesolo for your republic?' he asked. At all costs de Sanctis must be kept talking.

'Why did we choose Jesolo?' he said. 'Well, for one thing there was the ridiculous Free Jesolo Movement which has provided the perfect cover, but that's merely a superficial reason. The true motive is that it's the ideal place.'

'I find that hard to believe.'

'Have you ever read Pinocchio, Commissario?'

Even with the White Lady's hand on his shoulder, Peroni found himself taken aback by this question. 'Pinocchio?' he said. 'When I was a boy, yes.'

'You remember *il paese dei balocchi*—toytown—where Pinocchio and Lucino are taken with all the other boys by the genial coachman? There are no lessons there, no timetables, nothing but toys for them to play with from morning till night. And as they play, without their realising it until it's too late, they are turning into donkeys to be put at the service of the genial coachman. Well, Jesolo is the perfect *paese dei balocchi*, only for adults of course. Nothing to do but play from morning to night—and there's nothing more propitious than that to predispose the human soul for invasion.'

He's frightened to kill, Peroni realised in a sudden intuition. He worked up his courage with Pernod before coming, and now he can't quite screw himself up to the point of pulling the trigger. He keeps on putting it off and snatches at questions as an excuse for doing so. But for how much longer?

'Wouldn't Rimini have done just as well?' he asked.

'Oh no,' said de Sanctis, 'For one thing it's too big and for another it's too closely linked up with the rest of Italy. Jesolo's the right size and to all intents and purposes it's isolated. Taking it over was scarcely more difficult than taking over an island. And then Rimini's got roots in time, and where a place is rooted in time it's always more difficult to cut people off from their racial traditions which is what we need to do. Jesolo is perfect from that point of view, too. The village has a certain negligible history, but the lido is totally rootless.'

Those ravings of de Sanctis had their own nightmare logic, but they just didn't fit with waking reality. Maybe he and his friends did want to found the kingdom of Satan on earth, but there had to be more to it than that. Something he wasn't saying. But there wasn't time for cool reasoning about what that something might be. He had to be kept fuelled with questions, more questions—anything to keep him talking.

'But what about Venice?' he said, 'Venice is only just across the lagoon, and it would be hard to think of a place more rooted in time than that.'

'Exactly,' said de Sanctis, 'that's yet another reason that makes Jesolo the perfect place for us. We need *our* roots in time; if we didn't have them we would be cut off from our supply lines. So the vicinity of Venice is essential. But it *is* also across the lagoon—just far enough away—'

With shocking unexpectedness the door of the room opened and, if hearts could leap, Peroni's would have leapt at the sudden hope of rescue.

'Get out,' said a voice which Peroni recognised instantly and which eliminated all hope, 'I'll do it.'

Now Peroni understood what it was that he had felt was wrong. De Sanctis wasn't the man to organise and carry through a scheme such as the one he had outlined. He drank too much. He was weak. He was a showman of charm and extravagance, but he lacked the cold mind and the pure ruthlessness that the undertaking required.

But Marco, his charming son with the mass of tousled gold hair, possessed all the right qualities.

'Poor Papa,' said Marco. 'He's a man of parts, but he lacks tenacity. It always has to be me who does things like this in the end.'

For the second time Peroni felt the mouth of the gun against his body.

'It needed somebody like you,' he floundered in desperation, 'to run your father's organisation. But what happens when I'm dead? You'll have nothing left to argue with.'

'Oh, it won't be hard to get something. Half a dozen foreign

208

holiday-makers held hostage—*that* should make the government move.'

'And kill the goose that lays the golden eggs? Precious few citizens will come to your kingdom of Satan on earth if you start kidnapping holiday-makers.'

'Ah, so Papa's been piping his metaphysical tunes for you, has he? He does tend to go on about it just a trifle too much, don't you agree? Personally, I believe neither in gods nor devils, but I have no objection to him indulging his fancy—particularly since it's he who's paying for the fact.'

'The fact?' echoed Peroni dully.

'The fact, Commissario,' repeated Marco. 'Black gold. There's a fair-sized lake of it right beneath us now.'

So that was it—petroleum. Even in his present hopeless situation, Peroni couldn't help being awed at the revelation. Jesolo an oil field!

'How can you be so sure?' he asked.

'I'm reading geology at university,' said Marco, and Peroni remembered the report which had referred this fact, even using the adjective "brilliant". 'My thesis is on the location of petroleum,' Marco went on, 'and I'm putting forward a new system, a revolutionary system capable of locating petroleum in certain areas where hitherto it was considered to be totally lacking—areas like Jesolo where it's always been believed there was nothing more than a little methane. And though my professors don't know it yet, I've put this system to the test right here underneath their noses! I started the experiment working with a seismograph and explosive charges in the ground behind Jesolo lido to find out the type and depth of the rock formation.'

Peroni remembered old Rita's bombs and the reports of explosions received by the police.

'Then I started putting my system into practice and it came up with a one hundred per cent positive result. I've checked and re-checked and there can be no doubt about it. Jesolo is an oilfield. And there was Captain Gigi with his scheme for taking the place over! All we had to do was revive that scheme and make quite sure it worked this time. And it is working! Just as soon as the government agrees to Jesolan independence and we have the signatures on paper we can start drilling.

'That's how things stood when you came along, Commissario. If you had got wind of what was really going on *before* we got those signatures then everything would have been ruined. Papa said he'd take care of you—and the curious thing is he was really enthusiastic about having you as one of the faithful. You would have got all you were promised, you know, and you'd have had your position in the new republic. But no. For some futile idealism you were hell-bent on the difficult task of kicking yourself in the teeth. And you've achieved it, Commissario, you've achieved it.'

The aims of father and son might be different, but they both liked talking. And just suppose, thought Peroni, that the police are searching here, that within say five minutes they'll be in this house. Then keep him talking for five minutes.

'What makes you think you'll win?' he said. 'The Italian government has got tough lately. It's had to.'

He heard Marco laugh. 'You're trying to make me put it off like you did with Papa, aren't you? But you should know better than that with me. I'm going to kill you, Commissario. Now.'

There followed the most violent explosion Peroni had ever experienced and he felt himself hurtled over the chasm at last. It seemed strange that he should be face to face with the White Lady at last when they had walked together for so long.

Then it seemed even stranger that his thought should be continuing.

And not his thought only. Events also were continuing about him. Events of some considerable violence—shooting, struggling and shouting—which he found hard to explain.

It took Peroni an endless second to realise that, not only was he not dead, but he was in the process of being rescued.

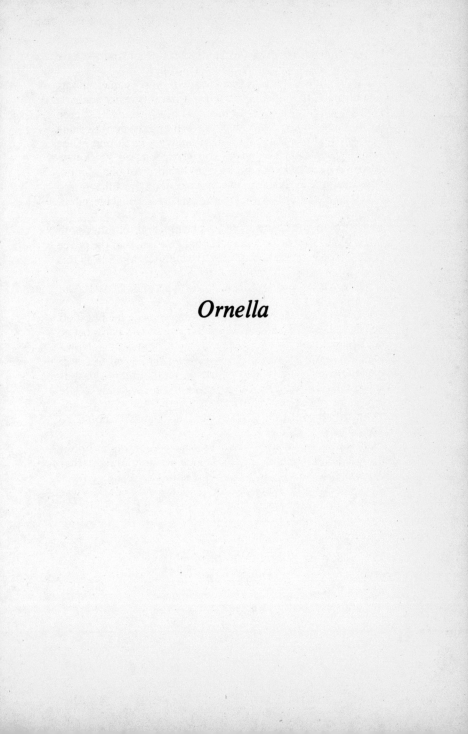

Ornella

Twenty-seven

Desdemona was overjoyed to see Peroni.

'She's never looked back since you gave her that Parmesan cheese,' said the vet. 'I've never seen a cure like it.'

'There's one more favour I'd like to ask you,' said Peroni, trying unsuccessfully to look modest. 'I'd like to—er take Desdemona out for a while.'

'Of course you may take Desdemona out, Commissario,' said the vet. 'I hold her in charge for the police.'

'Will I be able to—handle her?' asked Peroni who, in spite of her evident rapture at his presence, was still diffident of his powers as an animal handler.

'Oh yes,' said the vet. 'I'll put on her harness and lead, and you'll find she's no trouble at all. Just be careful not to keep her out in the cold air more than is necessary—she might catch a chill.'

In fact a damp and chilly end-of-September fog had fallen over Jesolo that morning. And it was that same fog which, a few minutes later, prevented anybody from enjoying the spectacle of the Rudolph Valentino of the Italian police driving down the main street of Jesolo in his red Alfa with a monkey sitting rapturously beside him gnawing a hunk of Parmesan cheese.

More than thirty-six hours had passed since, acting on a tip from an anonymous female caller, a police raiding party had erupted into the Jesolo prison where Peroni had been on the point of being shot by Marco de Sanctis. That raid had brought about the catastrophic collapse of Captain Gigi's republic. The arrest of Marco and his father had all the effect of pulling a rug smartly from under the feet of the Free Jesolo Movement. Its supporters everywhere were either being arrested, fleeing or trying to argue they had nothing to do with it. Some of the names involved promised an interminable chain reaction scandal.

The oil news had predictably rocked first the national and then the international scene, and already experts were pouring into Jesolo with all the impetuosity of one of their own gushers. Peroni felt curiously indifferent to this aspect of the affair, being more concerned with the problem of which it was only a sensational by-product.

He had been taken to hospital where a thorough check-up had revealed no serious damage. Earlier this morning he had been discharged, and was now trying to untie what looked like the last knot of all in the Kehzia murder tangle.

From his hospital bed he had set in train enquiries with the American army which had produced the information he had expected. But of itself, that wasn't enough. Nor was a love letter written over a quarter of a century before, however clear an indication it might offer. Something more solid was needed.

Peroni had pondered this while in hospital and had come to the conclusion that there was one long-shot possibility which involved making a fool of himself with Desdemona once more. The fact was that on the previous occasion he had established some form of communication with the monkey. He had, he believed, got his question over. But how could he expect her to answer it in the back room of a veterinary surgery?

The advice of the old man in Naples had come back to him. 'If ever you want to know something from a monkey just ask. Ask and go on asking. Sooner or later they'll understand what you want and they'll find a way of telling you.' That was where Peroni's mistake had lain. '*They'll find a way of telling you.*' Not *tell* you in sudden miraculous Italian, maybe with a Tuscan accent, but find a way of telling you. How could poor Desdemona find such a way closed up in that back room? But in the surroundings in which she had lived and Benito Mussolini had died it just might be a different matter.

The season was coming to an end and, with an odd mixture of reluctance and relief, Jesolo was putting itself away for the winter. As he stopped the car Peroni noticed that the boutique

on one side of Benito Mussolini's shop was already closed while
the bar on the other was in the process of closing.

Mindful of the vet's instructions he unlocked the door of the
photographer's before hurrying Desdemona through the brief
stretch of damp and chilly fog which lay between his car and the
shop.

Once inside he lit a black market English cigarette to give
himself countenance, for even when you are unobserved it can
be disconcerting to take the plunge into conversation with a
monkey.

'Desdemona,' he said, 'who killed him? You were here when
it happened. You saw whoever it was. Try and find some way of
telling me, Desdemona.'

She looked at him with her head cocked on one side and a
slightly puzzled expression as though he were speaking a
language she had once known, but now forgotten.

'Who was it, Desdemona? Who killed your master? Who
killed him?'

Now her expression seemed to say that she was on the brink
of comprehension and trying with all her simian power to cross
that brink.

'Who killed him, Desdemona? Who killed him?'

Suddenly the monkey gave an excited leap causing Peroni,
who was still not entirely confident in her company, to give a
nervous one. Her leap was only the start of a wild and alarming
performance. Having leapt, Desdemona proceeded to race,
chattering loudly, about the shop and its back room. In and out
she went at top speed, swinging on the furniture, climbing up on
anything that was climbable, picking up everything she could
handle and then throwing it down again.

Peroni was just wondering whether he should telephone the
vet for help when Desdemona came to a temporary rest on her
chair in the front of the shop. She did not sit in it, however, but
plunged upside down into it with her head where her bottom
should have been. Then after a couple of seconds she emerged
from the chair with something in her paw which she threw
triumphantly at Peroni.

Stooping to pick it up he saw that it was a photograph.

215

The photograph showed Kehzia Michaelis seated at a restaurant table with a glass of wine in one hand. Beside her, with an expression of tenderness which was anything but brotherly, sat the seminarian, Luca Zambelli. And in the background, slightly behind them with an expression of an altogether different nature, was the author of the love letter. Teodorico Bo.

Ornella was singing to a thin, end-of-the-season audience when she saw Peroni come in and sit down at a table. His presence put her in a fix. She was determined he would never have to feel obliged to her. For that reason she had made her telephone call anonymously and sworn to herself that he must never find out the truth. So now she tended to lean too far in the other direction and tried to avoid him when the group of songs was over. But he intercepted her.

'Will you have a drink with me, Signorina?' he asked.

How she would have jumped at the invitation a week before! And even now, she told herself, she'd be a mutt to turn it down. 'Thank you, Commissario,' she said.

'I thought you'd like to know,' he said when she had her drink, 'that the business of Kehzia is cleared up.'

'Oh?' She let her voice express no more than polite interest.

'She was killed after all.'

'Oh.' Something else she would have received differently a week ago. And now? Well, presumably her death would leave a vacuum in his heart which, as she had been taught at school, nature abhorred. And if there was a vacuum in his heart then just perhaps . . . She cut off the train of thought as though it had been an untidy thread hanging from her skirt.

'Oh,' she said and then, realising it was the third time in succession she had made that particular remark, she added, 'Can you tell me about it?'

He plainly not only could, but was bursting to, and the knowledge that she was providing him with an appreciative audience made her feel slightly more comfortable.

'She was killed by Teodorico Bo, Don Zaccaria's sacristan.'

'What?' There was no need to feign amazement. 'That funny

little man who takes the hat round in church?'

'The same.'

'But whatever for? I always thought he was so pious.'

'In fact, that was one of the reasons, I think, why he did it.'

'Killed Kehzia because he was pious? No, I'm just not there, Commissario. I'd better keep my mouth shut and let you do the telling.'

'Well, as a matter of fact it was you who first put me onto the right path, Signorina.'

'Me?' The news was as delightful as it was incredible. 'How?'

'By telling me about Luca.'

'That nice young man? You don't mean to say that he was involved?'

'He was indeed, very deeply. He was the cause of the whole thing.'

'Commissario, I'm baffled. Oh, I'm sorry—I said I wouldn't interrupt, didn't I? Just ignore me.'

'When you first told me about him, I naturally considered him a suspect. Then, when I was satisfied that he didn't kill Kehzia, I mentally dismissed him altogether, and it wasn't till two days later that I started to make detailed enquiries about him. If I'd done that immediately, the whole thing would have been cleared up much sooner.'

He admits to a mistake, she thought, rather as a millionaire might admit to mislaying a postage stamp.

'When I did finally enquire about him, I immediately noticed two slightly unusual things. First, he was born in Jesolo village. And second he's illegitimate. Nothing wrong with one or the other, but they set me worrying. So I spoke to an old woman with a fruit and vegetable stall behind the lido who had lived in Jesolo village and knew all the scandals there. And sure enough she told me the whole story of Luca's birth. It was the result of an affair between a local girl and an American serviceman. And she said this American was called Michele. Well, so he could have been, but it occurred to me that she just might have got it slightly wrong—that it wasn't his Christian name at all, but his surname. Michaelis.'

Ornella felt her eyes widening at this. 'You mean—Kehzia's

father?' she said.

'Exactly,' said Peroni, 'The dates fit, and when I had a check made with American army records yesterday I found that Michaelis was stationed here at the right time. He must have fallen in love with and seduced Luca's mother, then gone back to the States. And some years later he got married as a result of which Kehzia was born.'

'Making her Luca's half-sister?'

'That's right. But unfortunately I'd no sooner got onto this than I was kidnapped. So I was faced with the practically inescapable conclusion that the affair had some bearing on Kehzia's death or disappearance. But what? Why should somebody kill her or get rid of her because her father had given Iolanda Zambelli—that was her name—an illegitimate child all those years before?'

Oh, how he's enjoying himself, thought Ornella; like a little boy opening his Christmas presents. In fact if it wasn't so interesting I could switch off the sound altogether and just watch him for the sheer pleasure of it.

'At this point, however,' Peroni went on, 'I had a stroke of luck. While I was being held by the Free Jesolo Movement, at a certain point they moved me, and while I was being taken into my new prison, just for a second, I heard you singing in the distance, and I knew I was in Jesolo.'

She didn't quite see the link-up, but glowed with inward delight just the same.

'The next day, as a result of fiddling about with one hand that wasn't quite so tightly tied up as the rest of me, I came across a sort of little alcove in which somebody had left a box. The two men who were guarding me looked at it—I had sticking plaster over my eyes—and I understood from what they said that it was some girl's box of souvenirs. And the souvenirs included a letter which one of the men read. When I heard that it began *My dearest Iolanda*, knowing that I was in Jesolo village, I thought it just had to be Luca's mother. But it was when they came to the end of the letter that I realised I had come upon something of real significance—even though I thought I should never be able to do anything about it. The letter was signed Teodorico. Then I remembered that the old woman with the fruit and vegetable stall had said that somebody was in love with Iolanda Zambelli before the American arrived. And as the name Teodorico is hardly common, there was good reason to believe that that somebody was Bo.

'From the passionate tone of the letter, it was not hard to believe that he could well have been consumed by hatred for his rival. But there was a difficulty. Would even such a hatred as that unleash itself so many years later on the daughter of the rival? It seemed unlikely.

'But then I remembered two other things. First, the photographer, Benito Mussolini, was murdered and his shop was twice searched for a photograph which must have been very compromising indeed for somebody. And second, Luca's only known relative is an uncle. That made me wonder. I wondered whether the uncle might perhaps be in inverted commas, and I wondered whether he might be Teodorico Bo.

'If that were so then everything was explained. After Iolanda's suicide, Bo transferred his passionate love for her onto the only thing in the world that was left of her—her son. As Luca grew up, Bo continued to keep in touch with him. And then quite unexpectedly in his late twenties Luca announced that he wanted to be a priest.

'For a man of Bo's deep piety this must have been miraculous. Here indeed was God writing straight with crooked lines. From the illicit union so many years before, from Iolanda's suicide, from Bo's own wrecked life there now arose, phoenix-like, a vocation for the priesthood.

'Of course I was only speculating, but I found out when I questioned Bo this afternoon that the truth was very near my speculation.'

Ornella noticed with maternal affection the unsuccessfully concealed expression of satisfaction at the complaisance of the truth.

'Then Luca met Kehzia and felt for her far more than the merely brotherly affection to which he admitted—so much so that his entire vocation was put in doubt. And one evening he invited his "uncle" to the Far West Pizzeria and sprang the surprise of Kehzia.

'The effect on Bo must have been truly cataclysmic. Here was the second generation of the same American family come to wreak its wanton havoc as the first had done. And at that precise moment—flash!'

'I beg your pardon?' said Ornella.

'Benito Mussolini. He arrived and caught the happy family scene with the uncle contemplating murder, the nephew apostasy and Kehzia—well, we shall never know what she was contemplating.

'The rest is easy. Bo broke into Benito Mussolini's shop, found the negative he was looking for (without realising that a print had for some reason I have yet to discover been quite fortuitously run off it already) and decided that he was now free to go forward with his plan to eliminate Kehzia.

'For a while he carefully observed her comings and goings. Then one evening, knowing that she usually caught a bus when she finished at the Dolce Vita to Piazza Nember and walked the rest of the way up to the lighthouse by the beach, he waited for her on that stretch of sand and, when she came, killed her.

'As for Benito Mussolini, he must have recognised Kehzia from the picture in the paper and realised that he, too, had taken a picture of her. He obviously linked that with the burglary in his shop, found the print, indentified Bo and tried to blackmail him. For which he got himself killed.'

It all seemed beautifully neat, but Ornella's intuition told her that Peroni was not entirely satisfied. 'What's the matter?' she said.

'Nothing,' he said. 'Why do you suppose something's the matter?'

'No reason,' said Ornella feeling miserable, 'I just had a stupid impression.'

Peroni sluiced Chivas Regal in his mouth and lit black market English cigarettes for them both. 'You're right,' he said. 'Something is the matter.'

Ornella felt a lurch of excitement. For this thoroughly southern male openly to admit that he was wrong and she was right was almost a declaration of love. The victory was

220

overwhelming, but she realised at the same time that she must
tread yet more warily than ever.

'Do you want to tell me?' she said. 'If you don't I'll just forget
all about it.'

'It's stupid really,' he said at last. 'I'm convinced of the truth
of everything I've told you, and yet I've got doubts. Bo admits
the whole story right up to, but not including the full stop. He
denies that he killed her. He says that she resisted, freed herself
and ran away.'

'Well, he would, wouldn't he?' said Ornella carefully. 'I mean
he's got to make some sort of defence.'

'Of course. But I've got an odd feeling that he *could* be
telling the truth. For one thing, where's the body?'

'In the sea.'

'Exactly. And a man like Bo, born and bred in Jesolo, would
know how to get rid of a body in the sea. But,' he blinked into
the golden depths of the Chivas Regal, 'the Adriatic in these
parts usually gives up its bodies.'

'Even if they're weighted?'

'Perhaps not.'

Ornella realised that he was more disturbed than he let on
and female instinct, pounding furiously, told her that he was
looking to her for consolation and easement. It was a curious
and delicate situation. If it had been a simple matter of cupping
a female behind in his right hand, she realised, he would have
taken the initiative in a seagull swoop. But as the gift he
sought was the entire range of her femininity he was hampered
and even awkward. The gift would have to be bestowed with
great care.

'Commissario,' she said.

'Signorina,' said Peroni, looking at her with hungry, but at
the same time uncharacteristically humble Neapolitan eyes.

'Commissario,' a third voice intruded with savage suavity,
'there's a telephone call for you.'

As Peroni walked towards the telephone his spirit was in a
turmoil of amazement. It was as though he had never truly seen
Ornella before. Kehzia had always stood between them so that,

while he caught the gist of Ornella's words, it was Kehzia's lips that he watched. And now Kehzia was there no more and he was seeing Ornella in a way he had only ever seen a very small number of women.

He regretted that the situation couldn't be solved by a night in the ancient and crumbling palace where he lived near the Venetian fruit and vegetable market. But it was no longer as simple as that. Besides, his sister's monotonously reiterated refrain about it being high time he found himself a nice wife had began to sound alarmingly convincing of late. And Ornella would make a perfect wife, of that he was certain.

It is disconcerting when love and marriage pounce out at you in sudden ambush.

'*Pronto*,' he said having picked up the telephone receiver.

'*Pronto, dottore.*' It was Roberti's voice. 'We've just had a report from the police in Toulouse which I thought you should hear about.'

Toulouse? It suggested nothing. 'Tell me.'

'Apparently they pulled in some sort of itinerant Greek student for questioning. He'd been found sleeping at the station and had no documents. Well, while they were questioning him he suddenly seemed to go completely mad. When they'd calmed him down a bit he pointed at a photograph of Kehzia Michaelis which they'd had stuck up there ever since we sent out the missing person's report on her through Interpol and demanded to know where she was. It seems that she joined up with him and a couple of other semi hippies who were hitch-hiking their way through France. Her or somebody very like her. They spent the evening together and shared their food and she sang some songs which she said she'd written herself. Then they all went to sleep in a wood some way from the road, but when they woke up in the morning, she was gone. He said he'd been looking for her ever since.'

'When was this?'

'Last Wednesday, *dottore*. Three days after she was killed. Or disappeared.'

'Was he sure it was the same girl?'

'He said it was. And he said she was American. But the police

222

in Toulouse say not to place too much reliance on the story because everything else he told them was pure invention.'

'But why should he invent that?'

'That's what I thought, *dottore*.'

'Thank you, *dottore*. We'll think about it in the morning.'

Was Kehzia alive after all then, thought Peroni, footloose and unofficial somewhere in Europe? If she was, he understood with sudden insight, she would always be appearing here and there only to disappear again shortly afterwards. For, alive or dead, Kehzia was a dream. Ornella was reality. As he walked slowly back to the table he wondered which of the two he would choose.

Or which of the two would choose him.

If you have enjoyed this book and would like to receive details of other Walker mystery titles, please write to:

Mystery Editor
Walker and Company
720 Fifth Avenue
New York, NY 10019